His Peace

His Guardians
Book 3

By
Ronna Bacon

Prologue

The darkness pulled itself in on her as she paced rapidly through the city streets. She could feel the rain and cold moving in and so wanted to be inside before it hit. She glanced around, hearing something, a sound she couldn't place. She could feel someone tracking her steps. She shuddered, hoping it was not him again. He had stood outside the hotel she had been staying in last night; she had seen him through her window. She had left there so quickly, she wasn't sure if she had even packed up everything. Moving had become second nature to her, trying to stay ahead of him.

What did she have that he wanted? Or who was it she had helped that he thought she shouldn't have? Maybe it was time to confront the ghosts from her past.

He watched as she scurried through the dark streets, looking over her shoulder. He had accidentally hit that can and sent it spinning through the night, startling her and alerting her to the fact she wasn't alone. He wanted his revenge on her and he would have it, one day soon. A sneer showed crossing the pockmarked and scarred face as the moon briefly peeked from behind the clouds, then a low cruel laugh burst forth.

She heard his laugh and knew he was out there. Please, Lord, she prayed, let me get to safety. You have promised angels around me. Let me feel their presence.

Chapter 1

Frankie Brennan, Riverville police detective, dropped his gym bag on the bench and then sat to fasten his runners. It was early to be at the running track, the sun just peeking over the horizon in all its pink and purple glory. He watched as two or three runners passed by on their way around the track.

Murphy O'Brien straightened up from fastening his own shoes. "There aren't many people here early, are there?"

Frankie shook his head. "That's why I like coming here at this time of day. You're fresh, it's not hot, and it's not crowded." He looked up as a female voice called to him.

"You're late, Brennan. I thought you'd be here half an hour ago."

"Not everyone rises as early as you do, Adriel. How many laps?"

She waved and laughed as she ran past, stride long and steady. Frankie just shook his head.

Murphy was watching her, assessing her, as he always did when he met new people. It was part of his job. He was on Rebel's Elite Security Team and reading people had kept himself and his team mates alive many times.

"Who's that?" he questioned as the two men took to the track.

"Adriel? That's Adriel Sullivan. She's the director for the woman and children's shelter here in town." Frankie took a sideways look at his friend. "Deirdre and I have gotten to know her quite well since she moved to town a few years ago, both personally and professionally." He hesitated a moment, watching the runners, continued, "She's had a lot of threats, some vandalism, and hate mail. She takes in as par for the course but I know it really bothers her."

Murphy nodded, his thoughts going back to his own childhood. He remembered the running, the fear, the living on the streets until his mother could find a place for them. He often wondered why she had waited to long to leave his father. He would never know now. He hadn't really heard what Frankie had said about the threats. Then, he caught his words and turned to him to ask him about them.

"How many laps already, Adriel?" Frankie's voice broke into his reverie.

She laughed again as she settled into a stride matching theirs. "If you have to ask, you don't really want to know. I'm almost done anyway. Another lap and I'm heading home."

Murphy listened as the two with him bantered back and forth and then watched as Adriel waved and headed for the street.

"She's still running?" Murphy wasn't sure he was seeing correctly.

Frankie nodded. "She is. She lives a couple of miles from here and for her, running is nothing."

"I can see that."

Heading back to the compound he called home, Murphy's thoughts reverted to the woman he had met that morning. Running the woman's shelter would be time consuming, he thought, but he appreciated how much many women and children it would help, but to have heard she had had threats, that was hard to take. As he climbed from his vehicle and headed for the conference room for the briefing his partner, Abe Finlay, would be holding, he pushed the thoughts of his past to the back of his mind. He couldn't afford to be thinking about that.

Adriel walked out her front door and headed for her vehicle, stopping when she looked at it. The front end was damaged and there was fluid running down into the street from underneath it.

Just what I need, she thought, as she pulled her phone from her pocket and called in the report. I don't have time for this today, Lord, so why did it happen?

She groaned to herself as she saw which officer had responded. It had to be Don Ellis, didn't it, Lord? I'll need your help today. He's had it in for me since his wife walked out and took their two girls. I had nothing to do with it, but he still holds me responsible.

Murphy had headed back into town with two of his team mates, Ian and Micah. At loose ends, they hadn't felt like cooking and knew Mac's cafe would be just the answer. Settled in their booth and waiting for their orders, Murphy glanced around. The cafe was packed with the lunch crowd. Seeing the door open, he narrowed his eyes and then nodded to himself. Adriel had just walked in and was looking around. He could see her shoulders slump as she realized there were no empty tables or booths.

Adriel was disappointed. She really needed some of Mac's good food, but it didn't look like it would happen unless she had takeout and that just didn't sit with her today. A wave caught her attention. Murphy! What was he going here? Gratefully she moved through the cafe towards him, greeting friends, but not stopping to talk.

Murphy stood as she neared and let her slide in where he had been sitting. Nodding at Ian and Micah, he introduced her to them.

"Mac got your order?"

She nodded, her strawberry blond hair swinging against her cheek. She didn't notice the three men glance at her cheek and then one another. Murphy shook his head at the two seated across from him. She hadn't had that scrape this morning, nor the scratches he could see on her wrists. Conversation swirled around her as she caught bits and pieces of the men's talk.

Adriel looked up with a word of thanks as Mac set their food in front of them. She nodded when he handed her a small paper package.

"Tell SuEllen thanks, Mac, though I don't know how she could have heard."

"SuEllen has her sources, and they're usually right. She'll want to talk to you at some point."

"Tell her I'll stop by one day when it's not so busy." She looked past him as he walked away. "Great! Just what I need. I should have gone for the takeout."

The three men looked at her in surprise, then at Riverville Police Chief Caleb Logan as he pulled out an empty chair and brought it to their booth.

"Not here, Caleb." Adriel stared out the window.

"Just wanted to make sure for myself you were okay after this morning. He's off the force for good now."

She stared down at her food, and then at Caleb. "Super! Now he'll really be gunning for me. Would you please let me out, Murphy? I've lost my appetite."

Caleb watched her stride rapidly away, then slid onto the booth seat by Murphy.

"What's that all about, Caleb?"

Caleb shook his head. "She made more of an enemy today that she had had. She had a deliberate act of harassment and vandalism directed at her today. Her car was taken and used in a hit and run this morning, returned to her driveway and all the lines that could be slashed were slashed. She didn't notice it when she came back after her run as she went in her back door but did when she went to go out. The

8

officer who responded assaulted her. He's had an unfounded grievance against her for a while."

Murphy could feel the anger rising within him. One thing he could not abide was violence against women or children. "So that's how she got the scrape?"

Caleb nodded. "Her security camera caught the whole thing. She tried to explain where she was when the hit and run happened, gave the names of who she was with, and before the officer's partner had confirmed it, she was handcuffed and shoved up against the house wall." Caleb looked at Murphy. "You're one of her alibis, you know."

Ian and Micah exchanged a swift glance, then centred their gaze on Murphy.

"Care to tell us about that, Murphy?" Ian questioned.

"This morning? About 6 o'clock?" At Caleb's nod, he continued, "She was on the running track, had been for quite a while. Frankie and I met up with her there. She wouldn't say how many laps she had run by that time, but Frankie figured about twenty. I know her car wasn't there. Frankie said she always runs to the track and back home." He stopped. "That's who she said for them to call."

Caleb nodded. "That didn't go over well. He thought she was using him to get herself out of trouble. Unfortunately, he let his anger get the best of him. She's filed a complaint against him."

Murphy shook his head.   "I don't understand how he could abuse his position like that. Did he really think she was lying?"

"He has an unfounded grudge against her, and no one can get through to him that's he wrong.   He's thrown away his career now. There have been too many complaints from others against him in the last few years. Today was the final straw."

Caleb stood.   "If she needs you as a witness, you'll be around, Murphy?"

"Absolutely."   Murphy sent up a prayer for his new friend, asking God's protection on her and for peace for her in the situation she found herself in.

****

He stood and watched Adriel stride down the street, deep in thought.   Arrogant, he thought. Arrogant! Condescending! Meddler! Destroyer of families! One day he would fix her and fix her for good.

Chapter 2

Adriel tapped the papers she had been working on together into a neat pile and slid them into an envelope. The grant application was done once again. She stood and stretched, realizing it was late afternoon and that she had been at her desk in the shelter office all afternoon. She walked through the shelter, greeting the women and children who were residents there, spending time getting to know each one.

"Are we totally fully now, Kate?" She found the senior staff on duty in the kitchen.

Kate, an older woman, looked up from the dinner she was working on for the residents. "We are just about. We have room for a couple, then we'll have to go to the secondary residence."

"Okay. I hate that we're so full, but I am glad God has provided shelter for these people." She turned. "Unless you need me for something else, I'm off. I've got the grant application to mail."

"No, we're good. Go home and put your feet up." Kate smiled at her friend.

"Not likely. I have to go car shopping at some point, and I hate that."

"Did they find out who took your car?"

Adriel shook her head. "No, they didn't. I have a suspicion who it was but no proof."

Kate's hands stopped and she studied Adriel. "You don't think he would, do you?"

Adriel shrugged. "He's capable of just about anything. Watch yourself, too. We really need to upgrade our security here. It was fine when we started but it can be better."

She walked away, lost in thought, her mind going through the upgrades they really needed to do. She turned from the window in the post office, moved to avoid the woman behind her, and walked into a solid body. She stepped back as hands came up to steady her.

"Careful there, Adriel. You need to watch where you're going."

She looked up into the dark brown, almost black eyes, of Murphy and smiled.

"Yes, I really should. Too much on my mind." She looked around. "What are you doing here?"

"I volunteered to mail some packages for the guys." He turned to walk out with her. "Ian and Joseph are waiting for me."

"Thank you for what you said to Caleb."

He shrugged, then hesitated before speaking. "No problem. You shouldn't have been treated like that. If anything happens again or you have any threats, come find me."

She looked up at him, startled at the tone of his voice. "What happened in your past, Murphy?"

He shook his head, staring ahead. "I don't talk about it." He looked down at her, seeing the care and concern in her blue, almost violet, eyes. "It's in the past."

"It may be in the past, but it's affecting you now." She looked across the street at the SUV and waved at Ian. "You need to go. Your friends are waiting for you."

"Can we give you a lift somewhere?"

She shook her head. "No, I have some errands to run, and then I need to go do some research on a new vehicle."

Murphy stopped her with a hand on her arm. "Let me go with you when you go car shopping."

She stared at him, started to shake her head in a negative manner, then stopped. "Why is that so important to you?"

He shrugged, not willing to say why.

She shook her head and walked away. Men, she thought, you just can't understand them.

"How's Adriel after yesterday?" Ian watched her walk down the street away from them.

"She's not saying. Her face looks a mess though. He did a number on her."

Joseph's puzzled voice came from the back seat. "Care to explain, Murphy?"

Murphy turned and filled Joseph in on what had happened. A dark look crossing his face, Joseph muttered under his breath. Murphy really didn't want to hear what he said; he figured it matched his own thoughts.

Adriel set her Bible aside. She had curled up on her couch, her Sheltie tight to her side. She stopped to ponder what she had read about peace. She needed that today. She felt so unsettled over what had happened.

****

He stood in her back yard, waiting for her to come out. She had to at some point. Where was she? She needed to pay for what she did. What happened to her yesterday should have shown her that no one was fooling around. But there she was, walking through town, not a care in the world. Whoever did that to her just didn't do enough.

****

Abe sat down in the plane seat next to Murphy. He studied his friend and now partner in the security business. It had been a good move, he thought, offering Murphy the partnership.

"How long have we known each other, Murphy?" Abe asked that in an idle manner, but he had a hidden motive.

Murphy turned to look at him and shrugged. "I don't know. Ten years, maybe more, I guess. Since before your Dad hired me."

Abe nodded. "That sounds about right." He watched Murphy's face. "What's going on?"

"What do you mean?" Murphy avoided looking at Abe.

"Since you met Adriel and with what happened to her, you've been different. Your past is weighing in on you again, isn't it?"

Murphy sighed, then agreed. "Every once in a while, something brings it back up. This with Adriel, it brought it back stronger than it has in years."

"She's struck a chord within you somehow, hasn't she?" Abe was secretly glad that Adriel had been the one. Knowing both of them, he felt they suited each other.

Murphy glanced at Abe, then centred his gaze on the far wall of the plane. He finally looked back at Abe. "She has. I just don't know where or how it will go."

Abe looked around the plane cabin, then back at Murphy. "God is in control, my friend. Don't forget that. And don't forget to pray for the peace you need right now. I know your heart and how you want to protect the ladies we meet. This lady, she's special."

Murphy stared at Abe. "Just what are you saying?"

Abe smiled and shook his head, refusing to say anything else.

Murphy watched Abe as he turned away to talk with Micah. Abe cared deeply about each of his team and made sure he was aware of what was going on in their lives. Abe had never said what had happened to him in the past, but

Murphy knew he bore a deep secret hurt that came out of hiding every once in a while. He prayed that one day Abe would have the peace he so needed.

Chapter 3

"What is peace?" Greg Evans' voice echoed through the silence his words had created. He searched the faces of his congregation, knowing some had the secret to peace, others didn't. "Peace means different things to different people. In the Bible we have many verses about peace. The words I want to leave with you today are the words of Jesus: My peace I give unto you. Go home, study His words, and find His peace."

Murphy stood outside the church after the service and looked around. He had been hoping to find Adriel and maybe persuade her to have a meal with him. He turned as two of his teammates and their fiancees, Matt and Sarah and Nathaniel and Elizabeth, approached.

"Come with us, Murphy. We're going out for lunch." Elizabeth stood in front of him.

He shook his head. "Not today."

"Yes, today." Sarah nodded towards their vehicle. "Adriel's coming, so you might as well."

He turned to where Adriel was standing and then shook his head, a smile in place. "I have the feeling I'm being set up."

"Who, us? Never!" Elizabeth asked in an exaggerated voice.

"Yes, you two." Nathaniel swung his arm around his fiancee. "Now, it's up to Murphy and

Adriel if they want to join us or not, though they are welcome to."

Murphy slowly approached Adriel, uncertainty in his bearing. She smiled and then shook her head.

"I take it you were cornered too?"

"I was. Do you want to join them or find somewhere on our own?"

She laughed. "It would serve them right if we did go off on our own."

He laughed as well. "It's up to you. We can go out on our own on another day."

"Are you asking me out on a date now. O'Brien?"

He looked down at her, a smile softening the stern lines of his face. "I guess I am, Adriel." He reached for her hand. "Come on, we'll let them have today."

Adriel sat back in Murphy's truck, her face flushed with laughter. "I'm glad you said we'd go. Those four are a riot when they're together."

Murphy smiled. "Those two ladies have worked wonders with Matt and Nathaniel. Believe it or not, they are really serious. Today was different." He looked over at her. "Thank you for coming."

She smiled. "No, thank you. I needed this. Life has been too busy and too serious for me for too long. I need to make some changes."

Murphy was quiet for a minute. "What kind of changes?"

She turned her head to study him. "One of them is my job. It's a really important and I love the people I'm helping, but I'm burning out. I need to branch out into a different area to help these ladies." She paused, sadness creeping over her face for a minute. "There's also some on the board who are influenced quite well by the media and the media does not paint a good picture of our shelter at times or of me."

Murphy nodded as he brought his truck to a stop in front of her home. "I know that only too well." He looked down at his hands, fingers tight around the steering wheel. "Mom and I had live on the streets for a while and ended up in shelters when we could. It wasn't nice and it was so hard for her. It took some time but she managed to find work and a place for us to live."

Adriel reached for his hand. "I'm sorry, Murphy. I know it hurts still. But that has helped to make you who you are. I wouldn't trade any part of you."

He turned to look at her. "You really mean that, don't you? Not many people know what happened or that my Mom was killed in a work place accident. Most people would run the other way when they heard what my early life was like."

He came around and opened the door for her, holding out his hand for her to take. He didn't drop her hand as she expected, walking her to her door.

He stopped and waited while she keyed in her code, looking around at her front step area. "You've done well for security here at the front. Is the rest like this?"

She nodded. "We had a security expert go over everyone's home when we set up the shelter security. Any new employee or volunteer gets the same done for them."

She motioned him in. "Just let me put Echo out and I'll be right back."

Echo, he mouthed to himself. Who was Echo? Then he nodded. He had heard the bark. Good, he thought, she has a dog.

When she returned, he spoke, "I need to get going. We heading out tomorrow for about ten days or so. Will you be okay?"

She studied his face and saw his concern. "I should be. There may be changes when you come back." She laughed at the expression on his face. "Don't worry. Nothing really life changing, at least I don't think so. I am really considering an employment change, so that may happen."

"Just be very careful, please? I don't want to lose you."

She stood in stunned silence as he dropped a kiss on her cheek with the scrape and then turned and walked back to his truck, his head turning as he scanned the area out of habit. What had just happened, she asked herself? She watched as he drove away, then closed and locked the door, heading for the back door and

Echo, her sable Sheltie. At least Echo she could understand.

Murphy shook his head. Had he really said that to Adriel? It was so unlike him, but he felt different when he was around her, more at peace, more at rest. He shuddered suddenly, feeling a presence near him that was evil. His eyes scanned the area around his truck as he drove. He saw nothing but he knew something was there.

****

He watched him as he followed the truck down the road. One day soon, he would take him out and she would be on her own. Then he would deal with her and her interference. She would pay for what she had done to him.

****

Adriel sank down gratefully into her easy chair and set her cup down on the small table beside it. It was done. She had made her decision, a difficult one to make, but the right one. Thank you, Lord, for giving me peace about this. You know I have struggled for so many months with this. It's in Your hands now. Lead and guide me as I move forward. Then her thoughts drifted to Murphy and a smile softened her face. She prayed for the safety of the team, particularly the man who was fast becoming important to her.

Chapter 4

Peg Brown pushed open the door to Adriel's new office. She looked around. Adriel was right. It did need work: paint, flooring, window treatments, definitely new seating.

"Adriel, it's Peg Brown. Where are you, dear?" Peg listened but didn't hear Adriel respond. That was strange as Adriel said she would be here and for Peg to stop by.

Peg walked through the reception area and towards what would eventually be the office areas. There was just a bare framework in place yet.

"Adriel, are you here?" Peg turned as she called, then with a gasp dropped her purse and moved quickly towards the form on the floor.

"Adriel! Adriel!" Peg dropped to her knees and shook her young friend. No response! With shaking hand, she felt for her wrist. A pulse, but ever so weak!

She scrambled to her feet and for her purse. The police department was only two doors down but she wouldn't leave Adriel on her own.

Eddie Brown, the senior detective, stood with his arm around his wife, watching as the paramedics worked frantically on Adriel. Peg was in tears, sure if she had come in sooner, Adriel would be all right.

Dave Allison, senior paramedic, turned to them. "Peg, she was like this when you found her?" Peg nodded. "Did you notice any food or drink around her?"

"No, I just wanted to make sure she was alive and then get her help."

Eddie narrowed his eyes as he watched Dave turn back to Adriel. "What are you saying or not saying, Dave?"

"She shouldn't be like this. Can you get a team looking for any food stuffs or any cleaning agents, anything she could have eaten, drank or touched?"

"Peg, can you go with the officer here? He'll take your statement." He watched her walk away and then turned back to Dave. "What are you saying, Dave?"

"I think she's been poisoned." Dave looked back at Eddie. "Can you have someone go to her home as well?"

Caleb stood at the doorway of the building, watching as his crime team scoured the building inside and out.

"What do we have so far, Eddie?"

Eddie shook his head. "Not much. We found a water bottle near where she was lying and sent it on to the lab. The team at her house is going through everything there. I had Ashling Bradley come for her dog."

Caleb thought. "Is it related to when she resigned, do you think? I hear the meeting got a little heated."

"It did. Ben Johnson's on the board. He said Adriel's contract expired at 10:00 a.m. on that day of the meeting and she was not offered another one. Only one or two people on the board were aware of that. She was calm the whole time, reminded them of what her contract said, and refused to speak or give any reports related to the shelter. When they questioned her, she simply said she was no longer their employee and that she didn't have to answer anything. One of the women on the board threatened a law suit, but Adriel's response was that there were no grounds, they needed to go back to their own paperwork and read what was there. She left then. Ben said it got really tense after that. The woman who "neglected" to forward the contract on has been placed in charge of the shelter." He stopped, weighing how to say what he wanted to say. "I don't think it will be as well run or as well thought of as it has been."

"I'm guessing I know who you mean. She's been pretty vocal in the media."

Eddie nodded. "That's the one. It will be interesting to see if the staff stay. No one really likes her that well." He turned as a female crime scene tech approached them. "Did you find anything else?"

"We have some video surveillance tapes to run. I think we caught someone breaking in before the security system went live yesterday."

"Let me know when you get the pictures. If you can get a name, I'll buy you and your husband dinner at the best place in town."

"Thanks, Eddie, but that's not necessary. I want to find who did this to Adriel. She helped a good friend of mine."

Caleb watched as the woman walked away. "That's what I hear all the time, how well liked Adriel is. Who would do this to her?"

Peg had been allowed into the ICU room where Adriel lay, under heavy guard. She stood at her friend's side and prayed. They had no real answers yet as to how the poison had been introduced to her, but they had managed to extract some of it from the remnants in her water bottle and her blood work and start treatment. Tears in her eyes, she finally left, heading for the church and the prayer group meeting even then.

The men were exhausted, Abe could tell just by the slow way they were moving. This security assignment had involved a very high-ranked government official who had resented having to have security around him on a family vacation. His family had not made it easy either. He and Murphy needed to sit down and go over the direction they wanted to take their team. Another assignment like this would not be on the books.

He pulled his phone out as it chimed. Caleb. That's strange. Wonder what's up, he thought.

"Caleb, you caught us just as we unloading our gear. What's up?"

"Are you somewhere you can talk in private? Without Murphy around?" Caleb voice was solemn as he spoke.

Abe's heart sank.   Please, Lord, not Adriel. "Give me a minute until I get into the office, then we can talk."   He walked rapidly across the compound and unlocked his office door. "Okay, now I can talk. What's up?" He sank gratefully down into his office chair.

"I just wanted to give you a heads up so you can talk to Murphy. I know he'll be heading in to see Adriel as soon as he can."

"That we both know.   So, what's the problem?"

"The problem is that someone tried to poison her yesterday." Abe's eyes slid closed in fear as he heard that. "Eddie Brown's Peg found her in time. Adriel is in hospital here and I have her under guard. No one's getting near her."

"Who? And why?"

"We're working on that.   We know it wasn't Don, he was out of town, unless he hired someone. She's made enemies over time while she was director of the shelter. Peg walked into her new office two doors down for the department building and found her on the floor."

"Wait."   Abe was shaking his head. "What do you mean, was the director? Has she resigned?"

"That's right, you missed it being away. The last shelter board meeting was quite heated, I understand. Adriel resigned that night and has set up an office as an advocate for woman and children. She's a paralegal as well, so is offering that service to women and children only."

"How is she now?"

"The doctors say if she hadn't been found when she was, she wouldn't be here today. They're still trying to figure out how she got the poison. They're not sure if it was something she ate or drank or touched. They found a residue in a water bottle she had been drinking from but they're not certain that was the only source. Whatever it was showed up in her blood work and in the water and they were able to counteract it quickly. Although I don't think she'll like to hear they pumped her stomach as a precaution."

"Ouch." Abe glanced up as he heard the door. "I'll catch up with you later. Let me know how the investigation is going and if we can do anything."

He clicked off his phone and set it on the desk as Murphy entered and dropped the paperwork on his desk. Abe watched the fatigue in his friend but knew that he would be heading into town as soon as he cleaned up.

"Murphy, have a seat for a minute, will you?"

Murphy turned at the grave tone in Abe's voice and paled. "Adriel?"

Abe nodded. "Sit. I just got off the phone with Caleb." Abe hesitated to continue, his eyes on his desk as he spun his phone around. He looked up to see the dread in Murphy's face. "She's alive, but she's been hospitalized. Did you know she was resigning from the shelter?"

"She mentioned feeling burned out and wanting to get into something different. What happened?"

"Peg Brown found her collapsed in her new office. She's been poisoned, how the officials are still trying to determine. Wait, sit." Abe watched as Murphy sank back down. "I'll take you in but you need to clean up first. You'll scare her if you don't. She's being treated, Murphy, and Caleb has her under guard."

"Who?"

"They investigating it still. They haven't made any arrests. Before you ask, the cop she had the run in with was out of town. Caleb's not writing him out of the picture totally." Abe watched as Murphy struggled to control his emotions. He didn't think he had ever seen him so upset as he was.

"Do they know how?" Murphy's voice was barely above a whisper.

Abe shook his head. "They're not even sure on that. They still running tests, I gather." He stood. "Come on, let's get you cleaned up so you can go to your lady."

Murphy stood at Adriel's bedside later, watching her pale face. He touched it lightly, then turned to pull up a chair beside her bed. He lowered the side rail and reached for the hand that didn't have the IV in it. He didn't see Caleb motion for Sue, the detective that had been sitting with Adriel, out of the room. His focus was on the lady who was becoming a big part of his life.

Once in the hallway, Caleb turned to Sue. "Has she said anything?"

Sue shook her head. "She's been either sedated or asleep the whole time, barely rousing. I can tell you one thing, though. She will not be happy to have Murphy here. She did rouse enough to tell me to keep him away."

Abe smiled. "She doesn't have much of a choice, I'm afraid, Sue. He's not going to be wanting to leave her side." He turned to Caleb. "Any word yet of what it was?"

Caleb nodded. "They've isolated the agent in the lab and have been able to start her treatment. She'll be able to go home in a couple of days." He looked back down the hall at her doorway. "We need to keep Murphy safe as well. If he's around her, he may well become a target."

Abe turned as well and studied the doorway. "And I'm sure he'll be there as much as he can. We have a lot of training time coming up, so he'll not be there as much as he would like."

****

He watched the hospital hallway. Someone had gotten to her and almost killed her. That's not what he wanted. He needed to have her alive. So who had it been? He turned and glared at everyone in his vicinity, scaring a young child to tears with the fierceness of his anger.

Chapter 5

Murphy gently set Adriel down on her couch, then stepped back. She was pale and shaky still, three days later. She nodded her thanks.

He stepped away, to let Sue in closer. Walking back out the front door, he stared around, feeling helpless at the moment. Ian stopped beside him.

"Has she remembered anything?" Ian was concerned about Murphy but also about Adriel.

Murphy shook his head. "No, or if she has, she hasn't chosen to share it with me. I know Caleb is still wanting to speak with her at length." He turned in a circle as he scanned the area around her house, studying the homes near her. "I can feel something, Ian, I just don't know what or who."

Ian nodded. "I know what you mean. Someone is out there." He looked back at the house. "Are you staying for a while yet?"

Murphy shook his head. "No, I'm heading back to the compound. We've got the night training coming up. Sue will get her settled and then stay." As he turned back to the house, Ian spoke again.

"Murphy, what's that over by the fence?"

"What?" Murphy turned to where Ian had pointed. "I don't like this, Ian. There shouldn't be anything there. There wasn't this morning when Sue and I stopped by."

Ian reached out and stopped Murphy from moving forward. "Wait, Murphy. We need to let Caleb and his men handle this."

Murphy nodded, frustrated that it seemed more was happening to Adriel.

Caleb walked towards the two men standing near Ian's SUV. His face was grim and tight.

"A bomb?" Ian voiced the thought of both of them.

Caleb nodded. "The squad is still checking it out." He stared at Murphy. "It had your name on it, Murphy. Care to explain?"

"My name?" Murphy stepped backwards, shock on his face. "I have no idea why it would."

Caleb studied him. "I didn't think you would, but I had to ask. Either it's because you're involved with Adriel or it's because of who you work for. The lab team will go over it to see what they can find. I'm not holding out much hope though."

Ian stared at Murphy for a moment, then looked past him. "Why Murphy?"

Caleb shook his head. "It doesn't make sense, but it does. Whoever is after Abe seems to be going after one or the other of all of you. Watch your backs is all I can say."

A sudden yell cut through the air, followed by a strong blast, throwing the men to the ground. Groggy, Caleb shook his head and scrambled to his feet, running towards the area where the blast had come from. He could hear the calls for the paramedics resounding behind him.

Ian yanked Murphy to his feet and shoved him ahead of him towards the house. "Inside! Now!"

Murphy stumbled as he tried to regain his footing, stunned by the suddenness of the blast. Ian shoved him through the door, quickly letting Sue know what had happened and ordering her to keep Murphy inside, that he was a target. Ian turned back to where Caleb stood, surveying the blast area.

"How many got hurt, Caleb?"

Caleb turned. "Three." Sorrow crossed his face. "One didn't make it."

Ian stopped, shock covering his face. "It was that strong a blast?" At Caleb's nod, he paled. "If it had been Murphy or Adriel that had found it...." His voice trailed off.

"I think Adriel was meant to find it. It went off as they moved it." Caleb turned as he watched the paramedics working on the two survivors. "I don't know if they'll make it, either. Who is this guy, anyway?"

Ian scanned the area, eyes probing the shadowed areas. He could feel the evil around him. "He or she is watching us. Why do we always assume it's a male?"

Caleb stopped, frozen in step for a minute. Then he turned to Ian. "You're so right, Ian. We always assume male, and we should know better.

Look at Joshua and Laycee and what they faced. It was a female that did that." He was referring to his brother, Joshua and his wife, Laycee, who had been faced with murder attempts by a female accountant in town. He sighed. "I guess I'll be setting up another task force. Eddie and Frankie are really going to be thrilled, given the work load they already have."

Ian nodded as they turned to walk back towards the road. It would be a long time before the area would be cleared and released. "I'll suggest to Sue we take Adriel out to Rebel's. At least there we might be able to protect the two of them."

He turned from Caleb and headed for the house. He opened the door and beckoned to Sue.

"It's not good, Sue. One of the bomb squad is dead, two others may not make it." Sue gave him a horrified look. "The package had Murphy's name on it. We're going to take them back to Rebel's. If you can get Adriel ready, we'll head out. Caleb knows." He looked back through the door at Murphy sitting slumped in a chair, staring at Adriel. "That's not like Murphy, Sue. Has he said anything?"

She shook her head. "And I have no idea what he will say when he finds out someone is dead. I've known him since college, both of them in fact, and I still don't know how he'll react."

Ian watched Murphy for a few minutes. Then he turned and pulled out his phone. "Abe, we have a situation."   He went on to explain what had happened. Abe agreed the best place for them right then was Rebel's.

Murphy looked up as Ian touched his shoulder. "Murphy, we're moving you and Adriel to Rebel's. We need to keep you two together and safe. Caleb and Abe agree it's the best move."

Murphy noted wearily and rose, turning to gather Adriel into his arms. She slept through the move and the ride out to Rebel's.

Chapter 6

Matt stepped back out of the bedroom Sue had settled Adriel into and walked over to Murphy.

"Murphy, were you hurt at all?" Matt quiet question broke through Murphy's thoughts.

Murphy looked up, a brighter look in his face. "No, just a few bruises. We weren't close enough to the blast." He looked past Matt. "How's Adriel?"

"She's still sleeping. Somehow she slept through it all, which is a good thing. She doesn't need that memory on top of what's going on?" He looked past him at Abe, standing in the kitchen doorway. "Come on, let's go get some coffee and food. Abe's waiting to talk with you."

Murphy took the cup of coffee he was handed but waved off any food.

"Walk me through what happened, Murphy?" Abe was shaken. This was one of the worst events their team had been part of.

Murphy shrugged, then gave a rundown of what had happened. "I didn't see the package, Abe. We stayed away so as not to compromise the area. Not that it matters now."

"It does, Murphy." Abe watched him, seeing the fatigue in his whole being. He looked up at Matt and nodded.

Matt touched Murphy's shoulder. "Come on, friend. Let's get you somewhere you can lie down. You're going to be sore tomorrow."

Murphy nodded. "Has Caleb said anything about how she was poisoned or who?"

Abe shook his head. "It's still in the preliminary stages. They found traces in a water bottle." He hesitated before speaking. "You knew she's had many threats against her?"

Murphy sighed, then spoke. "I figured she had had, without her saying anything. It goes with the position. Mom and I used to hear the threats when we would be able to stay in a shelter. Nothing like what Adriel would have faced." Murphy missed the shocked looks that passed over the men around him. None of them had ever known he and his mother had been homeless.

He rose and headed for the living room, settling down on the couch. He was asleep as soon as his head touched the pillow. Matt stood over him, watching and assessing, finally draping a blanket over him.

"How is he really, Matt?" Abe stood in the doorway.

Matt shrugged. "Hard to say, Abe. He's tough but he's always been so quiet about what's going on with him. He's one you can depend on in a crisis. Hearing a bit of what he went through, I can understand better why he's like he is." Matt moved towards Abe and they headed for the outdoors. "This has really hit him hard."

Abe nodded. "We need to find out what's going on. Have Gideon start an investigation into everyone, and I mean everyone, connected to them. If he finds any names, pass them on to that Jace who did the work for us a few months ago." Abe walked away, hands in jacket pockets, head down in thought.

Matt watched. This had hit Abe hard, he thought, not just the assignment they had come off. There was something else going on with Abe, and he wished he knew how he could help. Lord, the only thing I can do is pray. You're still in control.

Abe sank down into his desk chair and stared at the paperwork on his desk. He would get to it, eventually, he thought. He pulled the desk calendar towards him and studied the date. This date always hurts, Lord. Will the hurt ever go away? He pulled out his wallet and from deep in it, he pulled out a picture and studied the laughing face of the woman in it. He ran his thumb over it, tears in his eyes. Where was she, Lord? Is she okay? Please, let me move on. I need to, but it's like You're telling me I can't, not just yet. He tucked the picture away and turned to his paperwork, losing himself in it.

He looked up at a tap and the door, and Frankie entered.

"Frankie, what brings you out here? I don't like the look on your face, though."

Frankie seated himself, eyes on the keys he still held in his hands. "No, I don't like to be here either. We've found some evidence."

Abe spoke slowly. "About the bomb or about the poisoning?"

"Both actually. They're related, somehow, is what the lab is telling us." Frankie looked up. "Both Murphy and Adriel are targets. We working on determining why and from whom." He stopped speaking. "I hate this, Abe. How many of our friends have been targets now? It's like it's open hunting season on us. I went through it with Deirdre. I don't want to see anyone else go through what we did, but I can't stop it. Where is God in all this?"

Abe watched his friend intently, seeing the doubts and worry underlying his words. "I know, Frankie. I feel the same. Now it's hitting my friends and team mates. I have to wonder who will be next. Who is targeting me, trying to get at me through them? I can't put my finger on anyone who would go to this extent, although I am sure there are some out there. Gideon's researched it, so has Sidney, his former boss. They can't come up with a name." He stopped, eyes dropping to his desk and the calendar. "I have to be away for a day or two later in the week. I don't like to leave but it's something I have to do. Just remember God's still in control. He knows the plans He alone has for us and why we walk the course He chooses for us." Abe looked up to find Frankie's eyes steady on him. "No, I'm not saying where I'm going. It's very personal. Murphy should be back to normal by then. If not, talk to Ian."

Frankie nodded, pulling out his phone as it rang. As he spoke, his eyes shot to Abe's.

When he hung up, he ran his thumb over the case, lost in thought, not sure how to express what needed to be said.

"Just say it, Frankie. That's usually the best way."

Frankie sighed, not looking up. "We lost a second bomb squad member. That makes two murders now. Our guys are fighting mad." He looked up. "They don't blame you or your team mates or even Adriel. They just want the one responsible." He stood to leave and Abe rose to walk him out.

"We'll figure it out. My guys want him or her as much as you do."

"That's interesting that you mention a female. Eddie and Caleb have mentioned the same thing. That just widens the whole scope of the investigation."

"Keep me updated." Abe turned as Murphy walked towards them. "I'll fill Murphy in and let him know you'll be talking to him if I'm away and you need anything."

Frankie nodded and headed for his vehicle, a shiver running through him. He searched the area, eyes probing, not seeing anything, but he could feel the eyes on him, the evil penetrating through him.

Murphy stopped and watched Frankie leave. "How's the investigation going?"

"It's not, and we have another death." Abe watched Murphy shake his head. "I know, Murphy. Caleb will be likely sending someone out to speak with the two of you." He turned to walk away. "Don't forget, I'm away for the end of the week. Let's try and stay safe, okay?"

Murphy nodded, then walked towards the end of the compound. Right now, he needed to be out in the open, away from everyone, just by himself. He climbed the hill behind the compound and sat on his favourite rock and prayed.

Chapter 7

Adriel turned from Murphy in frustration. She wanted to go home and he was having no part of it, not letting her know why. She resented being treated like a child and that was exactly how he had made her feel. She ran from where she had confronted him and ran right into Ian.

"Careful there, Adriel. You need to watch where you're going." Ian kept his hands on her upper arms to help her get her balance back. "Where're you running to, or from whom?"

"I want to go home, and Murphy absolutely refuses to take me. I want Echo back." She looked up, distress colouring her features. "Does no one get it?"

Ian looked across to where Murphy stood watching, not making a move to come towards Ardiel. "Tell you what, I'll take you in and then we'll see from there. Go, get your things. You're not a prisoner here."

Adriel searched his face, then nodded and ran for the house. She would be back before Murphy changed his mind.

Ian was waiting by his SUV and opened the door for her. Closing it, he watched as Murphy approached. He went to meet him.

"She's really going home?"

"She is, Murphy. You need to understand something. She's been through a lot in her life. We've had some good talks over the last couple of days. Maybe you should talk to her too." Ian walked away and climbed behind the steering wheel.

"You two didn't have words over me, did you?" Adriel's voice was very soft, so soft Ian barely caught what she was saying.

"No, we didn't, Adriel. We know each other well enough that doesn't happen. He's not happy with you, but he'll come around. I suspect he'll be in today to see you."

She shook her head. "Tell him to stay away. If he doesn't understand today, I don't think he ever will."

"You need to talk to him, just like you did to me. He doesn't know your history. He cares for you, Adriel. I don't think I've seen him like this. He doesn't want anything to happen to you. Nor do any of the rest of us. You're important to Murphy and that makes you important to us."

She turned to him, wonder in her eyes. "No, that can't be right. No one would ever feel like that about me."

"Did your early life taint your self confidence and self respect that much, Adriel? I see a very beautiful, very confident, caring, warm lady sitting with me."

She shook her head. "It's an illusion I've worked hard to perfect, Ian."

He smiled and quietly disagreed with her. As he parked in her driveway, he reached for her hand. "Let me have your security codes and I'll go through the house first. Then I'll come get you. I'm locking the doors. Don't unlock them for anyone but me."

Started eyes met his. "You really think I'm in that much danger." At his silence, she sat back. "I'm still not moving back to Rebel's. I need my own space."

"Murphy will have something to say about that, Adriel. I have never seen him like he is with you. Be careful with his heart, please." He stepped from the vehicle on that word and walked towards her house, keying in her codes, and walking through. Sue had been as good as her word, the house had been cleaned after the crime scene team had finished. He had a feeling Adriel would likely want to repaint and he would make sure they all volunteered to help her.

He stepped out her front door, scanning the area, then looked down. A parcel sat there, addressed to her. Not again, Lord. Please not again. He scrutinized it, then stepped away, pulling out his phone. His eyes sought Adriel's through the windshield.

Pocketing his phone, he walked slowly towards the SUV. He didn't want to be the one to tell her that there was another parcel. Innocent parcel or not, chances would not be taken. He opened his door and climbed back inside, sitting silently, staring ahead of him.

"Ian?" Adriel's voice came softly through the vehicle. "What is it?"

He turned to her, not wanting to destroy her innocence any more, to destroy the safety and peace she had had in her home. He sighed. "There's a parcel on your front porch. It didn't come through the mail, and there's no return address on it."

Hand at her mouth, she shook her head, eyes full of fear. "Who? Who is it?" She turned to stare out the side window. Ian watched as her whole demeanour transformed.

Here we go again, Lord, another lady ready to take on an unknown foe. Help us to keep her safe. He reached for her hand and tugged until she looked at him.

"We'll figure it out. Eddie's on his way with the bomb squad."

"Take me away from here, Ian. I can't go through this any more."

"Where would you like to go?"

"Miles from here if possible. Somewhere I'll be safe and not have to deal with this any more. I've had enough in my life already."

Ian nodded, then looked out as he heard a car stop. "Wait until I talk to Eddie, then I'll do my best to grant your wish."

Ian set the SUV in motion and headed for the airport. "I'm taking you flying, lady. I let Murphy know you're with me, not was what happening. We'll deal with that later."

"Flying?"

He nodded. "We have a jet that we use for business, but I have my own plane. That's what we're going up in."

An hour later, she sat, staring down at the ground so far below, then at the clouds around them as the small plane climbed. Ian brought it up above the clouds and then steadied it at a set altitude.

"This is amazing, Ian." She was quiet, but he could see her relaxing.

"I like to get away every once in a while and just spend time in the air. I feel closer to God, almost as if I could touch heaven."

She nodded, then relaxed back against the seat. "Did Eddie say anything about the package yet?"

He shook his head. "No. He won't yet. It'll take time. I don't like the idea of your going back there. I don't want to be the one to tell Murphy what's going on."

"No, I don't want to tell him," she sighed, "but I guess I have to, don't I?"

Ian nodded. Silence surrounded them. He finally looked over. Adriel was either asleep or praying, he guessed.

He reached and touched her shoulder. "Adriel, wake up. Adriel." She didn't move, deep in slumber. He smiled, then reached to unfasten her seatbelt and gathered her into his arms, carrying her off the plane and placing her into the SUV, fastening her in. He shut the door and then stared around. He could feel the evil once again. How could that be? No one knew she was with him or where they had been.

He headed for the compound, eyes searching. No, there was no one there. So why did he feel like that?

Chapter 8

Murphy came towards the SUV as Ian pulled to a stop near the big house as they called it. The men's cabins were scattered around back further.

"Ian?"

Ian could hear the question in Murphy's voice as he climbed out. "Your lady's asleep, Murphy. Take her in and then come find me. We need to talk."

Murphy stood beside Ian. "Okay, Adriel's settled and still asleep. Care to tell me what's going on?"

Ian gathered his thoughts. He had just finished a call with Frankie. It wasn't the kind of news he had wanted to hear.

"Let's walk, Murphy. I just spent the last few hours with your lady up in my plane. It's the only place I could think of where she could relax and not have to worry about her safety." He turned to Murphy. "There was another package at her home. I had walked through and found it when I came back out. No, not another bomb, but it might just as well have been. Frankie won't tell me what the contents were or what the letter said, but it was a direct threat to her. Not related to you. Not related to what she's getting set up to do."

"Then who?" Murphy stopped, deep in thought. "It has to have be related to her time as director of the shelter."

"Maybe. Maybe not. How much do you know about her past?"

Murphy shrugged. "We haven't known each other long enough to talk much about that. She's very quiet where that's concerned."

Ian hesitated, knowing he had to break a friend's confidence and not sure he should. "Did you know Sue knows her from college?"

Murphy shook his head. "No, I didn't. Sue and I are friends from then, but I don't remember her having a friend Adriel."

"Sue calls her Elle. She always has."

Murphy walked forward deep in thought, then stopped. "Elle. Her friend she ran with. I never met her at all."

"That's who she is. Sue hasn't said much other than that Adriel was raised in the foster system and kicked out of her foster home the day she turned 18." Ian stopped walking and watched the look crossing Murphy's face. "You can't tell her you know. It would break your friendship."

Murphy nodded as he turned to stare back at the house. "That's why she's like she is with the women and children. It's to help make a difference in their lives. But how do we keep her safe, Ian? We can't be here or be with her all the time."

"No, no one can. The only one who can is God. There comes a time when all you can do is pray and trust. I would say this is that time for you and Adriel." A hand dropped to Murphy's shoulder, then Ian walked away.

Murphy watched Ian walk away towards his cottage, then turned back to the house. Gideon and Rebecca, Abe's sister and her husband, were there, Rebecca working on another coffee table book of her photos. Gideon had told him he was running down information for Abe. He hesitated to go in, not that he didn't want to, he wanted to be near Adriel, but he also needed to think. He sank into one of the chairs on the front porch and sat, deep in thought. A cup of coffee coming into his line of thought startled him. He looked up. Gideon stood there, then sat in another chair.

"Want to talk about it, Murphy?"

"I don't know, Gideon. I just don't know." He leaned back in his chair. "How do we keep her safe?"

Gideon shrugged. "It's really not up to you, is it?" At Murphy's glance, he continued. "The ladies in our lives have their own minds and wills. They won't stand to be wrapped in cotton wool and stuck away somewhere we can keep all harm from them. That's not life, any way. You can't smother them, it would destroy them. What I learned when Rebecca was going through what she did with her stalker was that I had to be there when she needed me, to support her decisions, to become the one she would turn to and lean on. It was easier for us, we were married." He stared towards the distance reliving the fight and flight he and Rebecca had been on. "Now, with Adriel, it's a different ball game. She's different than Rebecca. She's tough, very sure of who she is and what she wants. She'll deny that, but it comes through in how she deals with everything life throws at her."

Murphy nodded. "I know and that scares me, that she'll just walk into a situation and handle it without anyone helping her." He sighed. "I wish I could just take her away from it all."

"Doesn't work that way, my friend. She would eventually resent you and come to hate you. You need to work wit her on this, and pray that the good Lord keeps her safe when you're not able to be there." Gideon looked up with a spark of mischief in his eyes. "You could do what I did."

Murphy gave a bark of laughter. "We could elope, but I don't think her friends would let her. Besides we're not at that point yet. Now you," he pointed at Gideon, "God worked quick with you and Rebecca. You were both ready and the time was right."

"Murphy?"

Murphy turned at the soft call from inside the house, set down his cup, and rose to go find Adriel. "Thank you, Gideon."

"You're welcome. Just let me know when and where the wedding is, okay? You missed out on mine. I don't want to miss out on yours." Gideon sat back, a small smile on his face, then looked up as Rebecca's hand reached for his.

She drew him from his chair and out into the wilderness around them.

"Murphy?" The call came again.

"Right here, my darling." He walked towards where she stood in an uncertain manner in the kitchen. "What's wrong?"

She turned, distress in her face. "Why, Murphy? Why is God letting this happen?"

"Oh, my darling!" He reached and gathered her close to his heart. "I don't know, but I do know He's the one in control, not some man or woman who wants to destroy you."

She clung to him and he could feel the tears as they started. His black head down on her blond one, he just held her as she sobbed. Ian started to come in, took a look, gave a smile, and backed out. His turn to make dinner was tonight, but he doubted any of the men who were around would object to eating out.

Adriel finally leaned back and looked up at him. "Thank you."

He dropped a kiss on her forehead. "No problem, my darling. Any time you want to cry, come find me. I'll hold you until you stop."

She nodded. "I got a call from Eddie. I need to go in and talk with him and Caleb today. Can you take me?"

He nodded. "Go, get yourself together, and we'll head in. I'd like to hear what he has to say." As she turned to walk away, he caught her back into his arms. "Before you go, let's pray, okay? God knows what's going on and how we feel, but He likes to hear it from us."

Chapter 9

Caleb closed his office door and went to sit behind his desk, eyes scanning the people gathered in his office: Eddie, Frankie, Murphy, and Adriel. Sue he knew was just outside, waiting if he needed her for anything; Adriel was a good friend of hers. Lord, this is so hard. We have no answers, just questions, no facts, just clues that go nowhere.

"Well, Caleb, where do we stand?" Adriel didn't wait for him to speak. "Or do we?"

"Adriel, we'll get there. Just let us go through what we have, okay?" He watched for her curt nod, then continued. "Unfortunately, whoever this is has been very careful. He or she leaves no clues, nothing that we can follow up on. The package that Ian found on your front porch? Let's just say it was very gruesome, and no, before you ask, I'm not telling you what was in it, other than it was a direct threat aimed at you and you only."

Caleb watched as her face paled. "Who would hate me that much?" She snorted and added, "Other than one person I won't name and he has absolutely no grounds."

Caleb shook his head at her. "No speculation, Adriel. We need to find the facts and find them quickly. Whoever this is has already caused the death of two good men. I don't anyone else to die and that includes the two of you. Eddie, what do you have?"

"The bomb was set by an expert, I can tell you that much. The rest is sealed into evidence, Caleb, so I won't go into more details. There was a note that was attached. We have copies of it, thankfully. It was directed at you, Murphy, not because of your friendship but because of Abe. Now that's an interesting twist. Whoever it is has been following you and knew you were friends with Adriel, taking advantage of an opportunity there. It could just as well as have been Adriel or even her dog that found it. It was set to go off as soon as it was moved just a bit.

"Now as to who it would be. We have no information. Anything we could have gathered in gone. We need you both to be extremely careful from now on.

"The next issue is the box that was left on your porch, Adriel. It was directed targeted at you. There was a note inside the box. Again, I can't tell you what it said, but it was not pretty. Someone really has a hate on for you. It's not Don Ellis. We finally got through to him about what he's been doing and he's gone into treatment."

Frankie spoke up. "I've been running names, Adriel. Does the name Will Lewis mean anything to you?"

She looked up, shocked, then shook her head. "Sure, it does. He was my last foster father, such as it was. He was a joke." She wrapped her arms around herself as if cold. "They only wanted foster kids under 18. If you were over 18, they got no money. In fact, you had to be out of their house at 12:01 a.m. the day you turned 18. It didn't matter what the season or the weather was. It was a horrible place to live, but they kept getting placements."

Frankie gave a half smile. "Not any more. Someone reported them, just after you had to leave. They were removed as foster parents about three weeks later. Know anything about that?"

She just stared at him and didn't say anything.

"About what I figured. Good for you." Frankie turned to Caleb. "I've tracked them. They moved to the other side of the country. Not up to their own tricks. They picked up a new line of work, running drugs. I put a bug in the ear of law enforcement out there."

Caleb turned to Adriel. "Now, it's your turn. Tell us what you know, what you think and who you suspect and why. I don't want you to hold anything back."

She shook her head. "I don't know, Caleb. I have really no idea who it could be. Maybe I'm naive or trusting, but I don't view people as potential enemies or foes. It's not who I am. The only ones I would suggest would have been Don Ellis and those two board members. I have had confrontations over the years with disgruntled husbands and boyfriends and sons, but none that stand out as a suspect. And no, I will not give names. I know I am no longer with the shelter, but that trust still stands. I won't break that with the women I helped."

Caleb turned to Murphy. "What about you?"

Murphy shrugged. "You've talked to Abe. I can't think of anyone other than who he might have suggested. I have no one in my past who would be looking for me. "

Caleb looked down at the notes he had been making and those he had been given. Lord, we're going nowhere. Who is it, and where do we turn? And this time, please, don't give a name to Hannah.

"If there's nothing else, Caleb, I'd like to leave." Adriel had stood and walked to the door.

"No, there's nothing else. Murphy, a moment if you will."

Sue was waiting for Adriel. "Let's go see your building. I hear there's been some progress in it."

Adriel stopped. "There can't have been. I haven't been working there, and I've been the one doing a lot of it."

Sue just smiled, tucked her hand in her friend's arm, and led her away. "Come on, Elle, let's go see if the rumours are right." Sue nodded at Frankie, who was watching them walk away. Sue knew he would let Murphy know where they were, and that Adriel should be safe with Sue.

Adriel hesitated as she reached the key for the lock and withdrew her hand. "I'm not sure I can go back in there, Sue, back where I almost died."

Sue's arm came around her friend. "You can. You're strong enough to do that. Come on. I want to hear what your plans are."

Adriel unlocked the door and then turned off the security system, reaching for the lights as she did so. She turned and stopped in disbelief. The office reception was done, just as she had planned it. Sue stood just inside the closed door, a smile on her face and pleasure in her eyes as she watched Adriel move forward, hesitating to look around, and then headed for the back.

Sue could hear her exclamations of wonder and pleasure and couldn't hide the grin on her face.

Adriel came back in. "Who, Sue? Who did this?"

"You have many friends in this town, Elle, more than you know. They all felt you were treated poorly by some on the shelter board. I hear there have been changes on the board, new faces brought in."

"Oh, Sue, that's not what I wanted. I just wanted to make a difference and God told me it was time I moved on."

"Yeah, well, it looks as if your God decided it was time for others to move on to. As to who did this, Peg and Marg Johnson organized the volunteers, and that was a feat in itself. Ben Johnson looked after the donations and they were many. Sue, Matt's girl, did the electrical. Joshua, Caleb's brother, looked after the renovations and he had a time of it, so many wanted to help. Leith and Regan Bradley did your tile work for you." She turned as the door opened and Murphy walked in. "And Abe and his men were here when they could be. I don't think they told Murphy, Elle."

Murphy shook his head. "No one said a word. I like this, Adriel. It's so you. How did they know?"

"Elle used to talk when we were running, how one day she wanted to set up her own office. We used to bounce ideas back and forth. These are the best ones she had."

"That they are." Murphy turned to Adriel. "I think I missed having a good friend back then, Sue. I had no idea you knew Adriel."

"My friends know I keep my friends' names close and only introduce if I need to. You weren't ready to know her back then. Now you are." With that comment, Sue walked out the door.

Adriel started laughing. "Did Sue really say that?"

Murphy nodded as he walked towards her. "She did, and she's right. I wasn't ready to have you as a friend back then. Now, I am." He stopped in front of her and reached for her hands. "I would like to explore friendship with you, Adriel. I like what I know about you already. Will you be my girl?"

She studied his face and read his heart in his eyes. She nodded. "I would, Murphy. One step at a time, though. We need to find out who's after us." She turned, pulling him with her. "Come, see what they've done for me. I can't believe it."

Murphy studied the woman he was fast coming to love. "I can. You're an important part of our community, you know."

Chapter 10

Abe dropped his duffle bag in the hallway of his home and walked through to the kitchen. He was hungry and was hoping there were some leftovers in the fridge. He greeted Gideon who was standing at the counter, making coffee. He nodded when Gideon held up the coffee pot.

His meal in front of him, he sank down into his chair and studied what he had dished up. He wasn't quite sure what it was but it looked and smelled good.

"Adriel cooked. I can't remember what she called it, but it's good." Gideon sat across from Abe. "Are you okay, Abe?"

Abe nodded. "I am. It was a long trip, but I needed to go." He took a bite of his food, then asked, "So what has been happening around here?"

Gideon looked at his cup, not quite sure how to let Abe know what had happened.

"That bad?"

Gideon nodded. "Almost. Adriel tried to go home. Murphy refused to take her, so Ian did. He found another package on her front porch. Caleb's not telling us what was in it, but it must have been pretty bad. It was a direct threat to her."

Abe's fork dropped back to his plate. "Another one? No one hurt this time?" When Gideon shook his head, Abe sighed. "At least we have that to be thankful for. Has Caleb said anything at all that you know of?"

Gideon shook his head. "He talked to Adriel and Murphy, so they may have more to tell you. I haven't found out much more than what we talked about before you left. Whoever it is covers his tracks very well. Neither Sidney or I can find a trace. I talked to Jace at Tracker's and he's digging into it for us as well. So far, nothing"

"There's someone out there after me and going after my team. We need to find them. He's escalating in violence."

"I know." Gideon paused as he heard the front door open and close. "I suspect that's Murphy. He would have seen you come in." He stood. "Rebecca and I are off for a few days. She's got a call to do a photo shoot in the mountains for a friend's website. She's looking forward to that."

"Stay safe. I have no idea who this creep will go after next."

Murphy leaned back against the counter and studied Abe. "Successful trip?"

Abe shrugged. "It never is. Just something I have to do." He looked up at Murphy. "So tell me, what did Caleb have to say?"

"Not much. They don't know much or have much to go on. We continue as we are and hope no one else dies in the mean while."

"That's not like you, Murphy."

"I know. I'm just frustrated I guess. So, we have that assignment next week?"

Abe nodded. "It's close to home this time, thank goodness. Only a couple of hours away and only for the day. We could use a few more like that."

"Then let's start narrowing what we do and be more selective. We're getting the assignments we are because of your Dad and uncle. You've wanted to change that for years. Now's the time. So how do we do that?"

Adriel moved silently through the house in the early morning hours. She needed to run but didn't want to wake anyone up as she left. The sun was just peeking across the horizon as she slipped from the house and stretched. Breaking into a slow run, she headed past the men's cottages and to the open area past them. It wouldn't be as good as the track, but at least she was able to get out and get moving.

Micah stopped and stared as he headed for the equipment building. His eyes were right. That was Adriel. He looked up to scan the area around her. It seemed okay, but he was uneasy. Ian stopped beside him.

"Is that really Adriel?" At Micah's nod, he continued, "Someone's going to have to have a talk with her, and I don't think she's going to like what she's told."

"Let Murphy do it. She's his lady."

"Let me do what?" Murphy stood beside them, having walked up without them hearing him.

Ian nodded in the direction they had been looking. "Tell Adriel how unsafe it is even here. This is when you get to put your negotiation skills into practice."

"Gee, thanks, Ian. So glad you are willing to let me go talk to her on my own." Murphy shook his head at their laughter, then headed towards Adriel. She was not going to like what he had to say, he already knew that.

Adriel slowed her steps as she saw Murphy approaching, and her heart sank. No, dear Lord, no more. No more deaths. No more restrictions. I can't live like that. She stopped as he neared her.

"Good morning, my darling. You're up and out early this morning." Murphy's greeting threw her off. It was not what she had expected.

"I had to run, Murphy. I can't not run. You know how much it means to me."

He stopped just short of her, watching her face and the flicker of emotions crossing it. "I know. It's fairly safe here to run, and I know you like to run in the early morning. We just need to know where you'll be and when. That's all I'm asking."

Micah looked back at them as he opened the building door. "At least she hasn't sent him away yet. Wonder how long that will take?"

"I doubt she will." Ian gave Micah a shove through the door as Micah laughed.

Murphy reached for Adriel's hand. "Walk with me for a bit? I'm not dressed for running."

She turned and walked by his side, saying nothing. She wasn't going to make it easy for him, she decided.

"Adriel, there is something you need to understand. Yes, we are isolated and you are safe. But we still have open area around us and it has been breached in the past. I don't want that to happen to you, to have you disappear and not come back. My heart couldn't take it."

She said nothing, digesting what he had said. "Your compound was breached? How?"

"They came in through the hills and down over the rocks. We can't monitor every inch of the grounds, they're too extensive. Abe has hundreds of acres here, some forest, some lakeland, the hills and rocks you see around us, the compound area itself." He looked down at her. "It's just too vast to monitor every square inch. That's why if you're going to run, let one of us know. Even back here, someone could get to you. If one of us is with you, it would be safer."

She tugged her hand from his and walked away. "I'm not giving up my freedom, Murphy. Not one speck of it."

He watched as she broke into a run. That went well, he thought. Now he had to mend fences with her and he couldn't right now. He had duties he had to get to.

Abe looked up as Murphy entered the office. "I don't like that face, Murphy. What's up?"

Murphy shrugged as he paced the office. "I'm not even sure any more, Abe. There's an undercurrent I can feel, but I can't put my finger on it. Have you ever felt like you were standing on the brink of a falls, just about to go over, and you had nothing to protect you?" He turned to look out one of the windows. "I feel like something is just waiting to break open and that Adriel will be hurt by it."

Abe hesitated to speak. "I know what you mean, Murphy. Come. Sit. What makes you think that?"

Murphy didn't speak at first. "I just have that feeling and I can't even explain it better than that. I'm sure you heard we found her running this morning in the area behind the cabins. I talked to her, but she's not in agreement to giving up anything that removes any of her freedom. She's getting ready to run, I think, and I have no idea where she'll run to."

"She won't run far from you, Murphy." Murphy looked up, startled at Abe's words. "She knows you'll do your best to keep her safe, as will the rest of the team. It's the uncertainty of not knowing who or what. Caleb hasn't said anything else, and I know they're working on it, trying to solve it to bring closure to the two officers' families. Not to say, he wants to solve it for you two."

"It's a tough one, Abe. I wouldn't want to be the ones working it." He became silent, lost in his thoughts. He smiled. "Gideon had an interesting comment."

"And that would be?" Abe smiled, having already talked to Gideon.

"He suggested Adriel and I elope." Murphy snook his head. "I won't do that to her. She deserves the best and that wouldn't be it."

"Are you sure about that? Have you even spoke to her about that, or have you not got that far in your feelings for her?"

Murphy stilled, then looked up at Abe. "What are you saying, Abe?"

"Just that I don't think you've talked to her, if your feelings have gotten to the point you'd even make a comment like that. I know you think you're protecting her by staying as far away from her as your heart will let you, and that you're going to say you haven't know her for that long." Abe sat back, lost in thought for a minute, then he shook his head at his memories. "You two suit each other. Everyone around you sees that. Think about it, okay? I'm not saying you have to. And pray about it. I know Gideon spent a lot of time in prayer before he spoke to Rebecca."

Murphy stared at his hands, gripped together in his lap. Abe was right. He was hesitating but he didn't want to bring any more harm to her. He stood. "I'll think about what you said, but no promises."

Abe smiled as he watched Murphy walk out of the office, then turned his attention to his work. An unmarked envelope caught his attention. He stared at it, then sighing, reached

for his phone.   Caleb would need this one, he
thought.

Chapter 11

Adriel walked down the street in town, sandwiched between Ian and Murphy. Murphy held her hand, no longer hiding his feelings for her. She wondered who had talked to him, but he did make her feel cherished and loved, something she could never really remember feeling. She pulled to a stop, dragging Murphy back to her, as she read the listing on the concert theatre wall. She turned and headed for the theatre door.

"Adriel, we can't go in there." Murphy protested as she dropped his hand.

"Oh, I think we can. Come on, you two." She led the way across the lobby and to the huge doors to the theatre itself. They could hear the music better as she pulled the door open, music that took them back to days of being a teenage, when country music was so much better, Murphy thought.

Adriel stopped, her focus on the band at the front. Ian eyed her, then the band at the front, wondering what was up. Murphy's eyes were glued to her face, seeing something there he hadn't seen before, then turned back to the band. A loud whistle made both men jump, until they realized it had been Adriel.

The band stopped playing and the lead singer stared through the lights, trying to find them.

"There's only one person I know that whistles like that. Elle?"

"That's right. Evan! When did you guys get to town?" Adriel almost danced down to the stage.

Murphy shared a look with Ian and then both moved down behind her. She hadn't thought when she went forward, or even when she had entered the building.

Evan had jumped from the stage and caught Adriel in his arms, swinging her around.

"Is this where you're living now?"

She nodded. "I have for a number of years. What are you guys doing here?"

"We got a request to do a benefit show for that shelter you used to talk about directing. Obviously it wasn't you who asked." When she shook her head, he nodded. "Didn't think it was, even though I was hoping it was. We've lost touch, friend, and we shouldn't have."

She reached to hug him again and then greeted the others in the band. She felt Murphy behind her and leaned back into him as his arms came around her. Evan's eyes narrowed as he watched them.

"Murphy, this is Evan, a good friend from my teens. I haven't seen him in too many years. Evan, this is Ian over here. Another friend."

Evan reached to shake their hands. "The boyfriend?" She blushed and he laughed at her. "You always did like them tall, dark and handsome, you know?"

"Evan, shut up.   Now what are you playing at the concert?"   They were off in a discussion of songs they had both loved.

Murphy moved back to sit, Ian beside him, eyes not moving from her. Ian touched his arm and made a comment, then got up to walk around the theatre.   He felt the evil in the building and wanted to make sure it didn't come near Adriel or Murphy.

"I'll catch up with you later, Evan. We're needing to get moving. And no, I won't go on stage and sing with you.   I don't do that anymore."

Murphy caught her hand as they walked through the lobby, Ian on her other side. "We need to talk about you taking off on a tangent, my darling. At least for now." It was said with a smile, but Adriel caught the edge under it.

She sighed.   "I keep forgetting.   I just want my life back."

"I know.   We'll get you a better one." Murphy pulled her back to him.   "Don't go running ahead. We can't protect you if you do."

She stopped, eyes ahead, not saying anything. Ian, a few steps ahead, got the glitter of tears in her eyes and sighed inwardly. Here we go again, Lord. How do we keep her safe when she's fighting us? It's breaking Murphy's heart, Lord, and no one but You can help.

His eyes raised to Murphy, and then narrowed.   What was up with Murphy? Something was and he wasn't sure any of them would be ready for what was coming.

Murphy spoke up, eyes on Adriel. "Ian, if it's okay, we'll catch up with you at Mac's?"

Ian nodded and walked away, a small smile on his face. He had noted the store they had stopped inadvertently in front of. What was it Murphy had said about Gideon and Rebecca?

"Adriel, come, let's sit for a minute." Murphy led her across the street to the small park and drew her down beside him on a bench.

"What did I do now, Murphy?"

"Nothing, my darling, nothing but be yourself. And I love that about you." Her eyes flew to him, shock in them. He gently smiled. "It surprises you, what I said. But I do love you. And it scares me what you're going through. I know you're in God's hand and I have His peace about what we're both going through. But I just want you to know that I would love to spend whatever time God gives us with you." His finger came up to her mouth as she opened her lips to speak. "I know I've surprised you. Take time to think about it. We're in no rush."

She nodded. "Thank you, Murphy. I do need time to process and pray about this. But you know, Ian going to be expecting us to say something." At his puzzled look, she nodded across the street, a grin on her face. "Didn't you catch the store we stopped in front of, did you?"

He looked, then started laughing. "No, we're not doing what Gideon and Rebecca did." She gave him a puzzled look and he told her how he had watched as Gideon had proposed to

Rebecca in a jewelry store and that they had been married that very night.

"No, I don't think so, Murphy." Adriel rose from the bench. "Now, you need to feed me."

He rose and caught her hand. "I will. I'm sorry you won't be able to be at the concert tonight."

She shrugged. "Evan understands. We were in the same foster home at the end."

Murphy watched as she controlled the emotions so near the surface. "But you shouldn't have to miss out on times like this with friends."

"It's okay, Murphy. Now that Evan knows where I am living, he'll be back as will his band. They're all friends from the foster system, though that isn't common knowledge."

Caleb looked up from his paperwork as Frankie knocked at his door. Frankie shut the door behind as he entered, then sank into a char, frustration and fatigue evident.

"Where do we stand on the investigation, Frankie?" Caleb got right to the point. He wanted it solved and solved yesterday.

Frankie shook his head. "It's just so bizarre. Whoever it is has covered their tracks well. Nothing on the paper or the ink to indicate it's anything but what you can buy off a department store shelf. The wording too. It's strange. It's directed at one person and written in such a way that only that person would understand what was being said. Abe is at a loss with the last letter. He can't think of anyone other than who he's told us that would be after him or his team."

Caleb stared into the distance. "This isn't helping. What about the note that Adriel got? Anything on it or the contents of the box?"

"The blood in the box was artificial, and the lab can't give us more than that. The note, well, that doesn't help out either. It refers to events supposedly in Adriel's teen years that never ever happened."

"What?" Caleb was shocked.

"I asked her about them. She says they never happened. She even sent me to talk to the lead singer of that tribute band that's in town right now. He's a friend, grew up in the same foster home as she did. He says the same thing."

"So we have someone making up stuff about her and threatening her with that?" Caleb sat back and stared at Frankie. "What are your thoughts?"

"My fear is that this is going to leak to the media, and Adriel will feel she has to leave town."

Caleb pointed his finger at Frankie. "That's what we do, what we did with Elizabeth. We'll go to the media, laying out just enough that the perpetrator knows we have information but not enough that would escalate things. Work with our PR people. And go talk with Adriel. Murphy won't like it but we have to do something."

Frankie stood. "I know we do. I just had putting the ladies out there like that."

"You want to do what?" Murphy wasn't sure he had heard Frankie right.

"We're releasing a statement to the media, stating briefly what has been going on and that Adriel is the victim of lies and innuendo." Frankie didn't back down from Murphy.

Adriel stood and watched the two men. Who would win, she wondered? It wouldn't be Murphy, if she had any say in the matter.

"I agree, Frankie." Murphy spun to glare at her. "Quit with the glare, Murphy. The investigation is dead in the water. We need to do something to get it back on track, and if it means a statement goes to the media, then so be it. Do you have a copy with you, Frankie?"

He watched the two of them. "I do. I'll leave it with you and you can make any changes you want to it. We're hoping to hold the press conference tomorrow. I would suggest the two of you disappear somewhere for the day."

Murphy shook his head. "The team's out of town tomorrow. Can we put it off a day?"

Frankie stood, weighing the options. "No, we need to get it out there yesterday. Sue's around. She'll spend the day with Adriel."

Frankie walked out of the house, leaving silence behind him. Abe strode towards him as he headed for his car.

"How'd it go?" Frankie had given him a heads up on what was coming.

"About how you figured it would. Murphy's starting to smother her and that won't work. "

Abe agreed. "He is and he needs to back off a bit. I'll see if I can get a chance to talk to him, although Adriel is quite capable of that herself."

They looked up as the door opened and Adriel came out, looking around. She ran towards Frankie, paper in hand.

"Frankie, take me in to talk to your PR people, please?" He could see the distress in her eyes.

Before he could respond, Murphy spoke from behind her. "I'll take you, Adriel. Please."

She hesitated, then shook her head. "No. No way." She turned to him. "You're adamant you don't want this done. I get it, what you're saying. What you don't get is how this is affecting my life. Your life is going on pretty much as normal. Mine has been turned completely upside down, and I have no idea why God is allowing that."

Abe and Frankie watched as the two strong wills battled each other, then saw the softening in both. Murphy reached for her hand and she took it

"I'll meet you two in town." Frankie's voice had a slightly amused tone to it.

Abe shook his head. "You two!" He walked away.

"It looks as if we've been abandoned. Come on, let's get this over with."

"Are you sure, Murphy? You're supposed to be getting ready for your assignment tomorrow."

"If Abe had wanted me here that bad, he would have insisted I stay. Besides, I don't have much to get ready for myself other than my negotiation skills, and those I can sharpen with you."

She stared at him, mouth open. He tapped her chin to close it. She looked at him, tears close to the surface, then reached to hug him. "Thank you. You make me feel so cherished. I have never ever had that."

He hugged her back. "I know. That's my goal in life, my darling."

The press conference over, Murphy and Adriel headed for her home. She needed to pick up some more clothings and she wanted to gather some paperwork she needed to work on. He stopped her from getting out of his truck.

"Wait. I'll walk through first."

"Be careful, Murphy. Last time, there was a package on the step."

He nodded. "I know. But Eddie has had patrol officers driving by and walking the area just to find anything if there's anything to find."

He returned in a few minutes and grasping her hand, walked her to her door. She hesitated not knowing what she would be facing.

"The windows broken in the blast have been repaired. Joshua made sure everything was fixed that needed it. Just so you know, Sue gathered volunteers to clean and paint your home for you."

Her eyes flew to his. "She did what?"

He nodded. "She says she had a debt to repay to you that she never would be able to, no matter what she did. Any idea what she's talking about?"

She shook her head and crossed into the house, gazing around, her eyes round in wonder. "She's picked the very colours I would. How did she know?"

"Maybe from the paint chips you had on your kitchen counter?" He laughed. "Go, walk through your house, and get what you need. Then we'll go find your dog for you."

"There, that's the last of it, Abe. Anything else for the night?"

Abe shook his head. "Go find your lady, Murphy. See if she stayed out of trouble today."

Murphy smiled and headed for the door. "And don't think I didn't see your face when you opened that letter. We'll talk later."

Abe stared at the closed door, then turned back to the letter. He grabbed his jacket and headed for his vehicle. He was getting so tired of this, having his men and their ladies threatened.

Abe settled back into their van seat, another assignment completed. He was glad it was over, glad that they didn't have a long flight home. Luke was behind the wheel and once everyone was fastened in, headed for home.

"I like this, Abe." Luke said. "Out for the day and then back home."

"I know. It's nice for a change. We're working to that end, Luke, just takes a bit of time."

Gear stored away, briefing over, the men scattered. Abe headed for his office with Murphy. They needed to finish off their paperwork and then they were done until the next day.

Abe sorted through the mail as Murphy worked on finishing off the report. His hand still as he reached for the plain envelope. He gave a quick look at Murphy, then slit the envelope open. Lips clamped together to keep his exclamation in, he read it through again. Whoever was after Adriel knew she was staying at Rebel's. He laid the letter aside. He would need to go find Caleb or Eddie or Frankie.

Caleb looked at the letter Abe handed him. "Another one delivered to you, not through the mail?"

"I suspect they're leaving it with the other mail in the box. Everything gets dumped on my desk. Rebecca and Gideon have their own box

so they would never see it. I just don't get it,
Caleb. Who is this?"

Caleb shook his head. "Our press
conference really didn't get us further along in
the investigations. Just a lot of useless tips, like
always. Now, this."

Abe looked at his hands, then up. "How
do we keep her safe? Whoever this is knows a
lot about her and her movements. Murphy is
going to smother her and that won't work."

"No, it won't. I don't know, Abe. This
one has us puzzled. I have people working on it
as they can, but we have so many other
investigations on the go that we can't devote all
our time to this one."

"I know. I have Gideon working on it and
he's contacted Jace at Tracker's. No one is
getting anywhere. And I know she's not sending
them to herself, as some in the media are
suggesting."

Caleb shook his head again. "We'll keep
working it, Abe, that's all I can promise.
Somehow, we'll get the answers we need."

Abe stood. "I hope we do before anything
happens to those two."

Adriel stared at Abe, then turned and
walked away. "No way, Abe. I'm done. I'm
not staying packed away in cotton wool any
more. Find someone to take me home."

"Adriel, wait.   That's not what I'm
saying."

She spun and stomped back towards him, anger in her steps. "That's exactly what you are saying, you and Murphy. I can't live like that. I need to have some freedom or I'll be like some wild bird you have captured and imprisoned. I'll wither away and begin to resent both of you."

She whirled away from him, nearly running into Murphy as he stood and watched the two. He caught her arm and stopped her. "If you want to go home, Adriel, I'll take you. You're right, we are smothering you, and that's not fair to you." He kept his eyes on Abe as he spoke, and saw the moment he gave in and walked away. "Go, get your things. I'll take you."

She gazed up at him and then ran for the bedroom she had been using, determined to go before either one of them changed their minds.

Murphy walked across the compound to the office later that day, hoping to find Abe there. Abe looked up from his desk and then nodded at the chair across from him.

"Get her settled back at home?"

"I did." Murphy didn't continue, and Abe waited. "I don't like it, Abe. She's a target being there on her own. I know she's just going to pick up her life and continue as she was before this all started."

"I know she will. She feels she needs to take back her life." Abe paused, not sure how to continue.

At that point, Murphy's phone rang. He looked at it, then answered it.

"Why, Murphy? Why did you do it?" It was Adriel's voice, but it didn't sound like her. Murphy hit the speaker button so Abe could hear. Abe listened to the conversation that had started, then headed to find Micah.

"Micah, can you trace a call to Murphy's phone? The number and voice say Adriel but we're not convinced it is. Ian, do you have her number you can call her on?"

Ian nodded, reaching for his phone. He was soon speaking with Adriel, confirming that she wasn't the one on the phone with Murphy. Murphy had started to tape the call. Abe's next move was to call Eddie. He knew Caleb had been out of town earlier in the day with Hannah and his two boys.

Eddie took Murphy's phone and listened to the conversation. "I'll put some people on it but it's not likely they'll find out much. It's a spoofing call."

"Spoofing?" Abe hadn't heard that term before.

"Someone uses your number to call someone, but it's not who you think it is. The call is layered under numbers and quite often originates overseas. We see it in scam calls."

"Micah wasn't able to get very far with it, either."

"No, it's too well hidden at times." He looked over at Murphy, sitting on the edge of Abe's desk, face dark with anger. "Someone needs to calm him down before he goes to see her. Adriel will pick up on this right away."

Abe nodded. "Keep me updated on that, please. It just adds another layer to the mystery." Abe walked towards Murphy.

"You need to go see Adriel, Murphy. She is expecting you."

Murphy nodded. "I know. I just don't know how to face her after this."

"With prayer and God, you can and will. Come on, buddy. Go see your lady. They won't find out anything tonight."

Ian's phone rang, interrupting them.

"Ian." Adriel's voice was shaking. "I don't have Murphy's new phone number. I can't remember it. I can't get the phones to shut off like you told me too. As soon as they power off, they come back on."

"Adriel, this is what I want you to do. Take Echo and leave the house. Leave your phones. Do it now. Murphy's on his way in. I'll have Eddie or Frankie come for you."

"Ian, I'm scared."

"I know you are. Here, Murphy's right here. I'll bring him to you." Ian pointed to his vehicle. "I think she has another bomb set to go off, Abe. Call it in."

Murphy and Ian ran for Ian's vehicle, praying they would be in time.

Adriel grabbed Echo's harness, fastened it quickly and ran from the house. She kept running in the direction of down town. Lights coming at her sent her off to the side on the road into the darkness. The vehicle stopped, and a man exited it.

"Adriel, it's Eddie. Where are you?" She remained where she was, quiet and not moving. It didn't sound like Eddie. Lights coming up behind the vehicle sent the man back into the car and speeding away. This vehicle slowed and stopped. Adriel could see the police lights on it and with the light on inside, she knew it was Eddie. She ran towards the car, scooped up Echo and slid into the front seat.

"Someone else was just here and tried to get me to go with him. He pretended to be you."

Eddie shot her a fast glance as he spun the wheel and headed back for the department. "I'm glad you had sense enough to hide."

A sudden blast from behind them startled them.

Adriel looked behind her in shock. "That's my house?"

"I would suspect so. You did well to call Ian and he did well to get you out of there." He fished his phone from his pocket. "Here, call Abe, his number's there, and let him know I have you and we're headed for the department. Murphy and Ian can meet us there."

Chapter 13

Eddie keyed in his code for the back door of the department and then lead Adriel and Echo to Caleb's office. Caleb was around, somewhere, he thought, seeing the lights on. He directed her to the couch and shoved her down.

"Stay here. I'm going to find you something to drink and something here for Echo to drink out of. Don't leave this room." He pointed to the door. "I'm going to make sure no one but either Caleb, Frankie, myself or one of Abe's men can get to you." She started to speak and he shook his head. "Right now, Adriel, I'm not sure who we can even trust. How did that man know Frankie or I was coming for you?"

She stared at him, shock on her face, trying to absorb what he was saying. "Eddie." She made a move to rise.

"No, stay right there. Caleb's around here somewhere. I"m going to find him. Ian will have Murphy here soon, if they aren't already. They'll come find you. I'll leave word at the front to let them through." Eddie closed the door and stood for a moment, trying to absorb all that had just happened. He looked up to see Caleb heading his way and he went to meet him.

"Adriel's house was just blown up." Eddie's words caused Caleb to stop short and stare first at him, then at his closed office door.

"She's in my office?"

Eddie nodded. "I've told her only you, Frankie, one of Abe's men, or me will be allowed near her. Someone tried to get her to go with him tonight be pretending to be me. She was smart enough to stay hidden."

Caleb's head whipped around and he stared at Eddie. He then turned and headed for the conference room. "We've set up in here. Talk to Sue, she running it tonight. Let her know what you have."

"You should know that Murphy got a call from Adriel but it wasn't her. It was spoofing her number. Micah wasn't able to trace it very far. Our lab has the information, and I'll get Murphy's phone from him as soon as he's here."

Caleb turned keen eyes on Eddie. "Spoofing? That's a new one for us in an investigation. Whoever this is, is getting bolder and more inventive all the time. Do we have anything at all that's concrete?"

Eddie shook his head. "Not a whole lot. Whoever this is knows our procedures or at least police procedures well enough to know how to circumvent our processes." He stopped, running his hand down his face. "I don't like it, Caleb. I don't want another one in our department selling us out."

Caleb stopped in the doorway. "Talk to Sue. See what the two of you can come up. There has to be something there we're missing." He turned as he heard footsteps behind him. Murphy and Ian were heading his way, faces dark with anger and worry. "I'm going to have to head Murphy off until he calms down. It won't do Adriel any good to see him like this."

"Actually," Eddie reached to stop Caleb from moving away, "I think it would. It might finally get through to her what we're saying"

"Either that, or scare her enough she runs and faces this on her own. Murphy, this way." Caleb led them to an empty office and closed the door. "Sit."

"Where's Adriel?" Murphy was not backing away, not when the woman he loved was in danger.

"She's safe and tucked away right now. I'll take you to her in a minute." Caleb studied the man pacing in front of him, then lifted his eyes to Ian. "Eddie found her and brought her in. Just before he got to her, someone else stopped and pretended to be him, to get her to go with him. Your lady's smart. She stayed hidden until she knew it was actually Eddie." Murphy's eyes had locked on his. "Her house exploded tonight. Ian got her out in time." He looked at Ian. "I don't know how you knew, Ian, but your words moved her to leave the house. I haven't had a damage report yet. Frankie's working that."

"It exploded, did it? I didn't know for sure, but the phones weren't acting like they should. Someone had to have had control of them. Can we track that?" Ian watched Murphy as he spoke. Murphy's posture was stiff and he remained silent. Please, Lord, Ian prayed, get through to him.

"Eddie had Sue working on that with one of the lab techs. It's going to take some time."

"Are you sure she's okay?" Murphy finally spoke again.

"Physically, she's fine. Emotionally, mentally, that I can't tell you. Let me take you to her. Ian, Eddie's made it clear to her that only one of Abe's men, Frankie, Eddie or I are to approach her. He's drawn in a tight net around her. He's not sure who he can trust, given that someone knew he was heading to pick her up."

Ian looked down at the phone he had pulled from his pocket, then handed it to Caleb. "Check my phone out while you're at it. I was the one talking to her."

Caleb reached for it, hesitated a moment, then shook his head. "Are we going to have to check all our phones? At this rate, we'll all have new phones."

Murphy followed Caleb to his office, waited as he tapped, and then opened the door. Eddie had turned off the overhead light, leaving just the desk light on.

He stepped around Caleb to go to Adriel and stopped. She wasn't there. He spun to look at Caleb.

"Where is she? Eddie said she was here."

Caleb looked for Echo. "Echo's not here either. Don't tell me she went out with the dog."

"She wouldn't have, would she?" Murphy stepped to the door and looked. "I'll see if I can find her."

Caleb nodded. "You go to the front, I'll check out back. If she went out the back door, she wouldn't be able to get back in."

They met back in his office. "No sign of her?"

Murphy shook his head. "Where did she get to?"

"Where did who get to?" A quiet voice with uncertainty spoke from the doorway.

"Adriel, where were you?"

"Eddie didn't come back with water for Echo. She needed it. I had to go find her some." She looked between the men. "Did you really think I had run? Did you?"

Murphy reached to draw her into the office. "No, we didn't, my darling. We were just worried someone had taken off with you."

Caleb moved quietly away and closed the door to his office. It didn't look as he'd be getting to his paperwork any time soon. He went to find Frankie and see if he had any word on the explosion.

Murphy gathered Adriel into his arms. She stood stiff, not letting him gather her as close as he wanted to.

"Adriel, you need to understand something. I couldn't find you when I got here. Caleb told me what happened with your house and with Eddie. I was just worried."

She drew back from him. "Then maybe we need to stop seeing each other and go our separate ways. That way, you don't have to spend your time babysitting and smothering me." She glared at him, tears near the surface.

Murphy shook his head and gave her a small smile. "That will never happen, Adriel. You're too important to me for me to walk away from you." He reached out his hand. "Come, sit with me. Let's see if we can figure out who's behind this. There has to be something we're missing."

She studied him, then brushed past him and sat on the couch. Echo jumped up beside her and cuddled close. Murphy smiled. He would have to win the dog over somehow. He sat on the other end of the couch.

She stared into the distance, not seeing anything. "So, who is it? And why me?"

"That's what we're trying to figure out. We're getting nowhere. There has to be something somewhere we're missing."

She turned to stare at him. "I have no idea who it would be. And I'm not able to give the names for the ladies from the shelter. That won't happen."

"We get that, but that's the only thing we can think of that it might be." He stared at the closed door. "Where did you work before you moved here?"

She stared at him again and then paled. She started shaking her head. "No. It can't be. He wouldn't."

"Who wouldn't, Adriel? Who is this man?" His eyes probed hers.

She shook her head, hand to her mouth. "No!"

He reached past Echo and pulled her over to him, cradling her close. Echo grumbled and then jumped down to the floor, standing there glaring at them before circling and thumping down.

"Who is it?" He held her as she sobbed. "Adriel, who? Can you tell me?"

He felt more than saw her nod. Caleb had opened his door at that point and started to back out. Murphy motioned him in.

"Who is it? Adriel, we can't help you if you don't tell us."

"I said I would never speak his name ever again. He was in charge of shelters and abused his authority badly. We suspected he was involved in human trafficking but could never prove anything. The same with drug running. I heard he had move to the west coast."

Caleb's look tightened when she said that and he mouthed to Murphy to find out the town if he could.

"Do you know what town?" He waited as she calmed herself down.

"We heard Ocean City but no one would or could confirm that. We were just so glad to be rid of him. I left there just before he move on. He left devastation in his wake. The shelters were closed by the city council and as far as I know, they have never opened them up again."

Caleb had left when he heard the town and went looking for Frankie or Eddie. "What town did her foster parents move to?"

"Ocean something, I think." Eddie sorted through the paperwork in front of him. "Ocean City. Why?"

"We just got a link." Caleb explained what Adriel had just told them.

"How did Murphy get that out of her?"

"His negotiation skills most likely or else he just knows how to reach and pull the information out of her. See what you can find out." He turned to leave. "Let me know when you find out something. Now I have to figure out what to do with those two."

"Have fun." Eddie turned back to his papers, missing the look Caleb shot at him.

Chapter 14

Murphy turned his head as Caleb came back in.

Caleb shot a look at Adriel.   "She's sleeping?"

Murphy nodded.   "I think the adrenalin has faded. What are we going to do, Caleb? We can't keep going on like we hare."

"No, we can't."   Caleb sat back in his chart and contemplated the paperwork on his desk. It would have to wait until tomorrow, and that would make a very long day for him. "I'm not sure what we're going to do, Murphy. Whoever it is, they are very determined to destroy Adriel, first mentally and emotionally. I'm afraid they'll go after her physically next. She won't stand to be locked up. She's made that very clear to all of us."

Murphy sighed, then nodded. "I know. She's adamant that she needs her freedom. If we take it away from her, it will destroy her. But we can't have someone with her all day, all the time."

"Not unless you two get married." Caleb smiled as he said that.

Murphy groaned.   "What's with you guys? You're not the first one to suggest that. I told her only when she was ready and only if and when she was."

Caleb smiled again. "You're a smart man, Murphy. You'll get there with her." He looked at his paperwork again. "God will protect her, but He may lead her down a path we wouldn't want to see her go. Only He knows."

"I know, Caleb. I pray that it doesn't get as bad as I can imagine. You and I, we've seen too much of the world and its depravity. We don't want it to touch anyone in our lives."

Caleb nodded. "That's so true." He looks at Adriel, asleep in Murphy's arm. "Where are you going to stash her tonight?"

"Abe's for tonight. She fought us hard to go home today, and look what happened." Murphy stopped, unable to continue for the emotions roiling through him.

Caleb watched in compassion as his friend struggled to control those emotions. He finally rose and walked out, to let him have some time and privacy.

Adriel stirred, eyes opening but not focusing. "Murphy."

"Yes, my darling, right here."

"What are we going to do? Where am I to live now?"

"We'll figure it out. Right now, I'm taking you back to Abe's. It's where you need to be." She shook her head. "You've nowhere else to go, do you? Then come back to Rebel's with me."

She didn't say anything for a while. Then with a defeated tone in her voice, she said, "He's won. Whoever he is, he's won. He's destroyed my life." She buried her head against Murphy, and he felt the tears as they started.

All he could do was to hold her close and pray for her, his heart breaking for her. Why, Lord? Why is this happening? I used to have such peace about situations. Now, I don't, and I need that back.

She finally sat back from him and looked down at Echo. Echo was up, chin on her knee, watching carefully. Adriel's hand went to rest on the soft head of her dog, and Echo's tongue came out to lick her arm. Murphy watched the bond between the two.

"When do we go back?" The question was so soft, Murphy almost missed it.

"Soon. We'll do our best, my darling."

She rose abruptly and paced Caleb's office. "The best just doesn't seem to be working. Why is this happening, Caleb? Who hates me so much?"

He shook his head as the door opened. "I don't know, Adriel, but we're doing our best to find out."

Abe stood in the doorway and watched the two of them. Adriel turned to stare at him, then her eyes went past him and widened in shock. "Why is he here?"

"Who?" Abe turned to see who she was talking about, but there was no one there. "Who was it, Adriel?"

"A ghost from my past. Is he on the force here? Is that why I can't stay safe?"

"Who was it, Adriel? Give us a name."

She shook her head.   "No one ever believed me about him. No one ever will. Abe, can we leave now?"

Abe exchanged a glance with Murphy, puzzlement in their eyes. Who had she seen? Did it go so much deeper than they thought? Abe didn't relish telling Caleb that she had seen someone in uniform from her past.

"We're ready to go now. Eddie's taking you out the back door. Will Echo go with me?"

Adriel stared down at Echo, whose brown eyes were staring calmly back at her, then handed Abe the leash. "Go, Echo. Go with Abe."

Echo didn't move until the command was repeated, but watched over her shoulder as she moved away with Abe.

Murphy stood where he could watch her face and saw the defeat and devastation in it. He reached for her hand. "Come on, darling. Eddie's outside the door waiting for us. Let's get you somewhere we can keep you safe for the night."

She nodded. "I don't want to go out there, Murphy. He's out there."

"Who is out there, Adriel? If you don't tell us, we can't help you."

She shook her head, then moved to the door. Eddie was watching her, concern on his face. He had heard her comment. His eyes raised to Murphy's. Murphy shook his head.

"She thought she saw someone from her past, Eddie, but she won't tell us who."

"Who was it, Adriel?" Eddie's voice was gentle with his young friend.

"No, Eddie. I won't say. No one ever believes me about him." She walked past him towards the back door.

"Murphy, you need to find out who she saw."

"I know, Eddie, but I don't think she'll tell me. I'll see what I can do, but don't get your hopes up. I'll see if Gideon or Sidney has some time to run her contacts from the past and see if we can find out that way. I don't even know if she's said anything to Sue. Maybe check with Evan, from that tribute band that was here. He's a friend from her teens."

Chapter 15

"Has she said anything at all, Murphy?" Abe tracked Murphy down in the office. "Caleb mentioned that she saw someone."

Murphy shook his head. "No, and that worries me. She gone totally silent, won't even talk about anything." He leaned back from the computer he had been working on. "I don't get it, Abe. Who could she have seen?"

Abe perched on the corner of his desk and watched Murphy's face. "I don't know. That's the scary part. If we don't know, we can't protect her. "

"I get that, Abe. I just don't know how to get her to open up. I don't even think she'd talk to one of the other women who have been through this. She's just shut down." Murphy scrubbed his hands down his face, then looked at Abe, fatigue colouring his face. "I'm so tired right now, Abe, I can't even think."

"Then go, get some rest. You'll think better when you've slept. Micah said he was working on something and he's been in touch with Jace from Trackers. Sidney's involved as well."

"That's good, but somehow I don't think it will be enough." Murphy pulled the calendar over and stared at it. "We head out again in two days. How do I go?"

"You'll go because you have to. You'll go because she'll expect you to. And you'll go in God's strength,Murphy."

Abe watched at Murphy pulled himself to his feet and headed, not for his own cabin, but the big house. Abe nodded. He would have done the same. He sighed, then moved to his chair, looking at what Murphy had been working on. What were thinking, Murphy? What were you trying to find out? He turned and looked at the door Murphy had walked through, then back at the screen. Where was it Adriel said she came from? He picked up his phone and called Eddie.

He hung thoughtfully. That was interesting news Eddie had shared. He sat back and stared at the wall. How did they tell her that her former foster father had tracked her down and had tried to find someone to kill her? That he had failed to find someone in Riverville and had started looking elsewhere. Had he found someone? Abe shook his head. How did they leave on their assignment in a couple days? Murphy would not be wanting to go.

Abe turned back to stare once more at the door. Murphy! It would stand to reason that whoever was hired might well try to get to her through him. How did they keep them both safe? It had been proven tonight they would go to any length to harm or even kill Adriel. Abe shook his head, then turning back to his computer, pulled up some of the security websites he had access to. He would work a while and see what he could find.

Murphy stood at the patio door, watching as Adriel wandered the back yard. She had asked him to take her into her office, she needed to do some work, but at his hesitation, she had walked off and left him standing there on his own.

"Adriel out back?" Abe spoke from behind him.

"She is. She's not happy with me."

"What did you refuse to do?"

Murphy spun, surprise on his face. "I shouldn't have?"

Abe shook his head. "If you refuse to give her some freedom, you'll lose her and lose her forever. There has to be a compromise you two can come to. When we're away, I can guarantee you she'll be off here and in town. She won't stand to be mollycoddled as my Mom used to say. Work with her, Murphy." Abe hesitated to continue speaking, his eyes staring past Murphy.

"Abe, what did you find out last night?"

Abe's eyes returned to Murphy. "If I tell you, it will make you want to protect her even more."

"What did you find out?"

"Her foster father was here in Riverville looking to put a contract out on her. She did more than turn him in as a rotten foster father. She turned him in for drug running and dealing as well. That's why they moved away. Officials are now breathing down their neck out west, and he blames her. He somehow tracked her down here."

Murphy stood in silence, then nodded his head. "So he got someone on the force here?"

"Why would you say that?"

"I suspect he's been planning this for a while. It would make sense." He turned back to the door. "He couldn't find anyone in town, could he?"

"No, he couldn't. That's not to say he hasn't found someone somewhere else. And he has, if last night is anything to go by."

"How do we know it was him, thought?" Murphy turned back to face Abe. "How do we know that for sure? All along, it's like there's been more than one person. We know someone out to get me and to get to you through your team. Are they using Adriel to do that too?"

Abe shook his head. "I don't know the answers to those questions, Murphy. That's what we're working on. Eddie is adamant that no one other than the ones he named last night approach her. He won't even let Sue near her." Murphy's eyes shot back to Abe's. "He is trying to isolate who she is seen with so that we can know if anyone is around that we need to investigate."

"Abe, who does Eddie suspect? Surely not Sue." Adriel's soft words startled the two men. They had not heard her come back in.

Abe shook his head. "I don't think so, Adriel. Just as I said to Murphy, he wants to keep your contact with people to a minimum for your own safety."

"I can't live like that, Abe. When will people understand that?"

Abe raised his heads in a defensive motion. "Don't shoot the messenger, Adriel. They want to talk to you again today. And I know you'll want to go by your house at some time, but they haven't released the scene yet from either the fire department or the crime scene. Until they do, no one is getting in or out of that area."

She nodded. "I need to go to my office. I have to start working there and putting it off isn't acceptable. I can't help show the women and children they don't need to be afraid if I'm hiding out myself."

"We get that, Adriel. We really do." Abe looked past where she was standing and out the patio door, then back at Murphy, standing protectively beside her. "We just want you around in the family for a long time, that's all."

She shook her head. "What's with you two? I just want to live my live. I have God's peace that no matter what happens, it's in His hands and His plans and purposes. Doesn't matter what you two or the police this. It's what I'm doing. If you're on board, good. If not, that's your problem." She moved to walk away but Murphy's hands on her shoulders stopped her.

The two men exchanged glances, then Abe nodded and walked away. Murphy turned

Adriel to face him, then caught her hand and led her back outdoors. "Walk with me, please, my darling?"

She glared at him but walked beside him as he headed for the benches at the back of the yard. He pulled her down beside and just sat for a minute.

"Murphy, what are you up to?"

He turned to look at her. She couldn't read his eyes or his eyes. She narrowed her eyes. This must be his negotiator face she thought, the one he wore when he didn't want to give anything away. Okay, two can play at that game.

"Adriel, I know how much you feel stifled by the measures we're trying to put into place. I know how difficult it is to have your freedom taken away."

"Do you, Murphy? Do you really know?"

He looked at her, sadness in his eyes. "Not how you're feeling, but I see it every time we go out on an assignment. We've kept everyone we protected alive, but not without a great bit of difficulty at times. It's because of what we have seen that can happen...." He paused, unable to continue for a moment. He looked down as her hand covered his.

"And I'm not making it any easier for you, am I?"

He shook his head.

"You need to understand, Murphy. I grew up with nothing almost. I had no home, no one to call my own. That's what makes this so hard. Losing everything, including my ability to move around freely, that's what I'm talking about."

"We really do understand that, Adriel. I can appreciate it, having come from what I did." He looked at her and pulled her into a hug. "We'll figure it out, my darling, somehow or other." He felt her nod, then she sat back.

"But it's not going to change what you're planning. Keep me in on the planning, please, that's all I ask."

"We can do that as much as we can." He sat back, arm around her. "But let's talk of something else. Have you thought any more about our conversation in town the other day?"

"What, about eloping? Not happening."

"No, I don't want that to happen. You deserve every moment of that special day, including all the days leading up to it." He paused, then asked again, "Have you thought any more about what I asked? Will you be mine for life?"

She stared down the yard, studying the flowers coming into bloom. Then she nodded. "I have, Murphy, that I have. You have to be an Irishman with that glib tongue of yours. Yes, I will be yours for life."

He reached and turned her face to him. "Are you sure?"

She nodded. He kissed her then.

"I have something for you. You may not want it, it's old. An antique really." She watched as he reached into his shirt pocket. "It was my great-grandmother's ring."

She stared at the ring. "It's very unusual, but I think you have a story to go with it."

He nodded. "I do. This is a family heirloom. My greatgrandfather was a sailing captain, searching the world for goods to bring back to Ireland and sell. He was given a sack of precious jewels one day as payment. From them he chose the five stones you see here." He held up the stone to look at it closer.

"This is what my mother always said about what her grandmother told her. The story goes like this: Grandfather decided to have a ring designed just for her. He wanted the diamond as the centre with the four points of the compass to remind them that God was in control and they never traveled alone. The diamond in the centre was to remind them of the North star, the brightest star, the one sailors used to guide their ships by. It was also to remind them that God had to be centre in their lives.

"The pearl was to remind them of the parable of how the man sold everything he had to buy a priceless pearl. God considers us His priceless pearls. Grandfather consider his wife his.

"The sapphire was to remind them that no matter how far they traveled, they never would run out of sky. That's how much God loves us, and that's how much he loved her.

"The emerald was to remind them that God renewed them each day and gave them grace to live. It also reminded them they needed to renew their love for each other every morning.

"Now, to the ruby. You remember how it says in Proverbs about finding a wife and how much more precious she is than a ruby. Grandfather chose the ruby to remind grandmother that was how he thought of her.

"If you will wear it, my darling, I would be honoured. If not, we will find out that you will."

She shook her head, tears on her cheeks. "No other one, Murphy, just this one. I would be e one honoured."

Chapter 16

"Where do we stand, Eddie?" Caleb tracked him down in the conference room. He looked around at the paperwork spread out around the room.

"We have confirmation that it was a bomb planted in Adriel's house. How it was triggered, they're working on it, but they think through her phone somehow. They're analyzing everything they can pull from the scene. The lab's pulling her phone records. They said they had something interesting but haven't elaborated yet."

"What about the call that Murphy got?"

"They traced it as far as they can. It comes back to a pay phone here in town. No surveillance cameras in the area."

"That figures." Caleb then turned to Frankie. "So where are we with security for her?"

"No where. She absolutely refuses to have security. Abe and Murphy are still trying to get her to agree." Frankie stopped and shook his head. "I don't know if I should tell you what Abe told me."

Caleb stared at him. "What?"

"Murphy and Adriel got engaged today."

"What!" Caleb wasn't sure he had heard right. Then he threw up his hands. "Sure, why to! Add another wrinkle to the plot!"

Eddie watched Caleb walk away. "Guess he didn't see that coming."

"Not so soon anyway. You know, Eddie, Adriel is going to need some ladies to talk with. Why doesn't Peg go out to visit her niece and nephew and take Marg Johnson with her?"

Eddie smiled. "I like how you think. I'll take to Peg and see what we can arrange. Did he get her a ring yet?"

Frankie nodded. "Abe said it's quite the ring, an heirloom in fact. His great-grandfather designed it and it incorporates five different stones, in the shape of a compass." Frankie's words slowed as he spoke, a thought coming to him. He shoved back from the table he had been sitting at and headed across the room, searching through the piles of paper and folder for what he wanted. Finding it, he opened and scanned through the documents.

"What did you find, Frankie?"

Frankie handed Eddie the file. "This. I think we just found a lead we had overlooked. It was the thought of the compass ring that brought it back to my memory."

Eddie read through the file, then headed for the door. "Caleb needs to see this. It looks promising."

Caleb raised his eyes from the folder. "And this was just sitting there?"

Eddie nodded. "Until Frankie remembered it. It was Murphy's ring to Adriel that sparked a memory in him."

"Her ring, eh? That's an interesting connection, to say the least."

Eddie nodded. "Now we have to track through this and track down this fellow."

"Give the information to Tracker's. They can run it faster than we can."

Eddie stood and reached for the folder. "I'll do that. By the way, I'm sending Peg out to see Adriel. With this engagement, she'll need support and she doesn't have her mother."

Caleb stilled, then nodded. "Okay. Do what you have to. It's not what we would have chosen to have at this time, but what can we do?"

Eddie shook his head as he walked out of Caleb's office. Something was up with Caleb and he couldn't put a finger on it.

Murphy turned as Abe entered the office. "I think we're already to take off tomorrow. Paperwork's all ready and the men are too. They've loaded up everything we'll need."

Abe nodded. "Good. It's an early start, but it's not that long a drive. Thank goodness we have some local assignments now."

"I agree. I don't think we have any distant ones now on the books. We've refused them all, which I think is a good thing. The guys were getting tired of traveling."

"I was too, to tell you the truth. It was time to change how we work." He studied Murphy. "Just a thought. How do you think the team would feel about turning more towards training that actually being the ones on the front line?

Murphy sat back in his chair. "That's an interesting thought, Abe. What made you think of that?"

Abe shrugged. "I've been praying about a change in direction for us, and that keeps coming up."

"Run it by them after we get back. From the muttering I've heard from Matt and Nathaniel, they would like to be home more now that they're engaged. I'm sure the others are feeling that way too. Traveling like we do, it makes it hard to get to know any ladies and to get involved in a relationship. It's also hard on being able to keep connected with our church."

"That it is. Think about it and give me your thoughts about where you'd like to see us go." He stood and walked to the door when he heard a vehicle pull up. "There's Eddie. Wonder what he wants."

Eddie stood in the office and looked around. "I have some news but I'm not sure how to explain it."

"Start where you always tell me to, at the beginning." Abe smiled at him.

Eddie sighed, then sat in the chair beside Murphy and explained what they had found.

"An organization or an individual?" Murphy's first question threw him.

"That's what we're trying to figure out. Jace at Tracker's is working on it for us. He's set aside some other work to devote time to it. He's hoping to have some information for us by late night or tomorrow. I'll be able to contact you, Abe?"

Abe nodded. "You can. We're out of town, about four hours away, and gone for the week."

Murphy glanced at Abe, then at Eddie. "What do we do with Adriel? I know she's not just going to stay here."

"Now that, that is a real problem. Caleb is adamant about not allowing anyone else around her.   But I had a thought.   I hear congratulations are in order. I'm thinking that if Peg and Marg come out to see her and Ben comes to, that would take care of some of it. I'll be around when I can and so will Frankie. Gideon's back and will be working from home. You just need to convince her to listen to you and stay put."

"That's easier said than done." Murphy shook his head. "She has a mind of her own."

"Then set her up to work by phone from here. There's a safe room she can get to in the house if she has to. She can communicate with us from there." Eddie stood. "The only other option Caleb has come up with is to lock her away in jail, and that he's not yet ready to do."

Abe snickered. "I can see him trying to do that. It would never work. She's take off running and he would never catch her."

Eddie shook his head. "None of us would." He turned to point back at Murphy. "You're the only one she would let catch her."

Murphy shook his head at them. "On that note, I'm off to find her. Let me try and talk to her again. Losing her house may be enough to change her mind about the security here. But then again, it's Adriel we're talking about, and nothing is sure with her."

Eddie turned his head to watch Murphy walk away, then turned back to Abe, studying his nephew. "What's up, Abe? Something other than this is bothering you."

Abe signed, then elbows on his desk, scrubbed his hands over his face. "I don't know, Eddie. It's just that everything seems to be closing in on the team and on the ladies the men have come to love. Where do we stop it?" He looked up at him. "Does God even really care any more?"

Eddie studied him. "That is definitely not you, Abe. Your faith is strong, but this is letting it take a beating. My advice is to go to your Bible and read about God's peace. He has a plan for this, not what we may want, but what He is allowing to happen for His reasons. We can question Him but we need to accept that we may never ever know the real reason. Can you do that?"

Eddie waited as Abe digested that, then finally nodded. "But that's not all that bugging you, is it?" Abe's eyes turned back to him. "I know you take off every year, the same time of year, and disappear. You never say why or where you go. I'm not asking that. I'm just asking if there's something I can do for you."

Abe shook his head. "I'm trying to let go of something in the past, but it just doesn't go away. It's been so many years," Sadness covered his face. "I don't know that it ever will."

"And until it does, you can't move on with your life. Now I know how to pray for you. I wish you had told me earlier."

Abe nodded. "We're also talking of making changes here at Rebel's. With the men getting engaged and married, they don't want to be out of the road as much. Murphy and I are tossing around the idea of steering the company towards security training."

Eddie stared at Abe. "Now, that's what I like to hear. You're changing for what you want, not for what your father offered. It's about time."

"Which way would you take it?"

"The same way you're thinking. There are some many companies starting up in security, but there are very few with the experience you all have that could or would do the training."

Murphy headed for the house, hoping to find Adriel. He didn't see her and tracked down Rebecca.

"Where's Adriel?"

Rebecca turned, a smile on her face. "Hello to you too, Murphy." He groaned at the smile. "She was here a minute ago. Let me see if I can find her."

Murphy turned to watch Rebecca walk from the room and shook his head. She would never change. He turned back to study what she had pulled out for supper. Just maybe he could convince Adriel to go out for a meal instead.

"Murphy! You're back!" He turned as Adriel almost ran into the kitchen and into his arms. "You had a successful trip?"

"We did. Now, my darling, how would you like to go out for dinner? I think we should be safe enough?"

She shook her head. "Not tonight, Murphy. I promised Rebecca to help her with something for supper and I won't go back on my word."

"What are you two ladies preparing?"

"Don't ask, Murphy." Rebecca's voice raised his head. "She won't tell me what the name of it is, but it certainly looks interesting."

"That it does. If not supper, then how about a walk after dinner, just the two of us?"

Adriel nodded, then shoved him from the room. "You can come back when it's ready and not before."

Later that night, Murphy tracked Abe down in the living room. He sank gratefully into one of the easy chairs. "I think you have the right idea, Abe, changing us over to training. I put out feelers over the last few days, as I know you id, and the word coming back is positive."

Abe nodded. "That's what I'm getting from them, too. Let's work towards that. We'll need quite a few meetings but that's what we'll do. Gideon says it was quiet here while we were away. Peg, Marg and Ben were out a couple of times. Those two ladies have taken Adriel under their wings with respect to the wedding."

"That's what she said. Sounds like the planning is moving along. All we need to do is set the date."

"And why don't you?"

Murphy shrugged. "It's just that I would always feel as if I rushed Adriel if I didn't let her have some time to enjoy this part. And I don't want that regret to colour any part of our lives together."

Abe smiled. "You know best, I guess."

Before Murphy could ask him what he meant, Ian was at the door.

"Ian, what's up?"

"We've got a breach somewhere along the rocks. The alarm has gone off."

Murphy and Abe were on their feet. "Ian, the house is yours. Gideon and Rebecca have gone to town. Let him know. Adriel's in the office, I think. Find her. Be prepared to hit the safe room if you need too. Murphy, find our guys and spread out. They know, Ian?"

They heard his affirmative response as they hit the back door on a run. They knew Ian would keep Adriel safe.

"Adriel." She looked up at Ian's voice, started to smile, then dropped the paperwork she had been holding.

"Ian, what is it? Is it Murphy?"

He shook his head and held out his hand. "I need you to come with me now. I need to get you to the safe room. Murphy's fine, but we have unwanted company."

She reached for his hand and ran with him for the cellar stairs and down them. They could hear footsteps coming in the door. Ian reached for a shelf and pulled it towards him, shoving her through the opening that appeared first before following and pulling the shelf closed behind him and locking it in place.

"Won't they see the marks?" Ian could barely hear her whisper.

He shook his head. "No. It's balanced in such a way that it swings out and back without touching the floor. Unless you know where to touch or get lucky when you're feeling for it, you can't find it."

The light was dim, and she could barely see his face as he listened intently. Then he had her hand in his grasp again, leading her away from the entryway.

"We go out this way. It takes us out near the cabins. No one should be able to find us. Wait." He went back and grabbed a sweatshirt that had been left there not long before. "Pull this on and pull the hood up over your hair. The moon will reflect off it if you don't."

He stopped her with his hand before she could step out of the tunnel. He listened, then pulled her with him towards the cabins. He motioned towards the back of them as they ran. Finding the shadows at the back, he once again stopped and listened, shoving her behind him and against the cabin wall. His weapon drawn, he waited in silence.

Adriel jumped as a dark form appeared beside her, clapping her hand over her mouth before she could scream. A hand touched her shoulder, then the form moved forward beside Ian, handing him something. She watched as he settled the earpiece into his ear and nodded as he heard the quiet voices over the radio. They were connected again.

Ian listened to the quiet voices in his ears, eyes straining to see through the night. Joseph stood beside him, facing the other way, body in front of Adriel. They worked together well, usually teaming up on their assignments. As word came over that the men had left the inside of the house, they could hear their team members spreading out further. Ian touched

Joseph's shoulder and motioned towards the back of the compound yard. Joseph nodded and faded away.

Ian turned, bending low to her ear and whispered, "We'll follow Joseph. Come on." He reached for her hand and pulled her along, keeping in the shadows. Her breath came in gasps as she tried to keep up with him. He slowed his steps finally and stopped, shoving her behind him in the doorway of a building, which building she wasn't sure. He stood in front of her, eyes watchful, weapon ready and listened to the low voices of his team mates over the radio.

Joseph appeared once more, moving close to whisper. "They're out here somewhere. They didn't find Adriel in the house, so now they're searching the grounds. Luke took out one of them, but there are at least three more of them."

Both men drew back into the shadows as movement reached them. Matt appeared out of the darkness as did Luke. Quick low whispers and they were on the move again, this time deeper in the wooded area. The men kept Adriel between them, their bodies in the way of harm to protect her. Finally, they stopped, allowing her to drop to the ground in exhaustion.

Abe materialized out of the darkness. One by one the team members appeared. Adriel watched faces, then stared past them.

"Where's Murphy?" she whispered. "He's not here. Where is he?"

Abe spun, counting heads, then pointed silently back the way they had come. All but Ian faded away, back to search for Murphy. Abe's heart sank. He had a feeling they wouldn't find him, that he had been taken in order to get to Adriel. Quiet voices over their radio confirmed it. Nathaniel had found Murphy's weapon and ear piece but not him. He reported a disturbance on the ground but they would need to wait for daylight before they could see it properly.

Abe sighed, then called the team back to the house. The intruders were gone. He needed to contact Caleb and report Murphy's disappearance. The only problem, who was it directed at: Adriel or him? Both seemed to be intertwined right now to the point they couldn't separate the two.

Matt returned to the living room, exhausted as every other team member. He sank deeply into one of the chairs.

"Did you get Adriel settled?" Abe's quiet voice broke through the silence.

"I finally did. I called Paul Owens from the clinic down town. He suggested a sedative. It took a while to get her to agree but she finally did. I'm hoping she'll stay asleep all night. She's emotionally at the brink."

Abe nodded, then looked at the other team members. They were all hurting. They had had intruders before, but never like this. They had never really faced what they were facing tonight. They had been in danger before, had been and broken on assignments, but never had one of their own taken from their own home. God, You

know where he is. Keep him safe. Help us to
find him.

Chapter 18

Murphy was dumped carelessly to the ground near the van, the man not caring if he was hurt or not. He figured it didn't matter. Murphy won't be alive that much longer anyway. He was only useful to get to Adriel.

The leader nodded as the remaining men regrouped.

"We need to take him out. He can't be allowed to talk. You two, go after him." He sent two of the men back towards the compound, where they could watch for their compadre to be moved to town. He would never make it, if they could help it.

The leader motioned to Murphy. "Get him into the van. We'll dump him in the bin until we need him."

Murphy's body was almost thrown into the van, his head bouncing off the floor. The four men climbed in, sorting themselves out around the vehicle. He didn't hear it pull away from outside the compound gates, didn't see it pull over as the police cruisers raced for his home. It would be hours before he would even begin to take note of what was going on. Whichever man had taken him down with the rifle butt had succeeded better than they thought they would.

Abe met Caleb at the door. The men had exited to talk with the responding officers.

Caleb took a keen look at his friend, then hand on his shoulder, turned him back into the house and shoved him into a chair.

"Talk to me, Abe.   Tell me what happened."

Abe went through the night step by step from his point of view.   "We kept Adriel safe, but at Murphy's expense.   I know they wanted one of them to use again the other.   Or at least, that what's we're supposed to think?   What if it was Adriel they wanted, but there's something else going on with her that we don't know about?"

Caleb nodded.   "I had thought of that. Jace at Tracker's has been working on her background.   He hasn't found out much about her family other than they were good people. Her mother died in childbirth, her father drowned trying to save someone when she was about two.   There were no other relatives that he could find.   That's how she ended up in foster care.   She got labelled as a problem child from day one because someone didn't bother to take the time to do the proper assessment of her and place her in the proper home."   He looked closely at Abe.   "What do you know about Murphy's story?"

"I think he's told me about everything he can.   He doesn't remember his father, other than he remembers being scared."

Caleb hesitated.   "I don't want to go behind Murphy's back in telling you this without talking to him first.   Murphy's father was arrested for a homicide when Murphy was really young. He died of a heart attack before he even made it to the jail. Murphy and his mother were tossed out on the street by the landlord, illegally at that."

Abe shook his head. "I don't know if he is even aware of that. Does that have any bearing on what we're going through now?"

"Not likely. We're still trying to sort through the compass group that Frankie discovered. They've hidden themselves well, but somehow or other, Adriel has made a connection to them, likely through her work in the shelter, and doesn't even realize she has. It's a really nasty group, and her foster father became part of it on the west coast. We're still trying to sort out how far reaching it is."

"We really need to find them. The men that came through here were well trained. It was like we were tracking ourselves." Abe stopped. "Is the compass group the one that's been after me?"

Caleb shrugged. "We don't know that, but I doubt it. They're not into security and so far we can't find any link to anyone who you've worked for."

Abe nodded. "The men are really taking it hard, not just for themselves. They really hurt for Adriel. She's sassed them, talked back to them, taken on each one in turn, tried to run from each one of them, but she has endeared herself to them in one way or another. She doesn't even realize she has. They're also hurting that she's lost Murphy and we have no way of knowing where he is." Abe stopped, unable to continue for a minute. "We don't even know if Murphy's still alive, and that hurts, Caleb. It makes me doubt God and that He's in control, even though I know He is."

"He understands, Abe. You know that." At Abe's nod, Caleb continued, "Greg's got a prayer chain going. They're meeting round the clock."

He rose as Ian came to the door. "Abe, can you come out for a minute? I'll stay here in Adriel needs someone."

Abe and Caleb exchanged a glance. They stopped as they went down the steps, staring that the group of grim men standing in the middle of the driveway. "Is that your intruder on the ground, Abe?"

Abe nodded. "It is. Matt, what happened?"

Matt stood as Abe and Caleb approached. "Sniper. He never had a chance, never said a word to us."

Caleb looked around in the growing light. "He's good to take someone out in this light. They really didn't want him talking."

Abe shook his head. "How do we go up against someone like this?"

The team members looked at him, then at each other. This was so unlike Abe.

"We've talked about this, Abe. You know how and you know how we'll win."

Abe sighed. "I know. Sorry, guys, it's just gotten to me, just like it has with you. Let's say we meet up in about 30 minutes. We'll spend some time in prayer, then make what plans we can. Think about any possible scenarios that you can. Think of anything that you may have heard, seen, felt. Anything! It might just be the smallest thing that breaks this wide open. Look how Adriel's ring triggered it with Frankie to look for that file and start tracking down that compass group." Abe turned and walked away, heaviness in his steps, shoulders drooping.

Murphy stirred, rolling onto his side, his hand fumbling for his head, holding the side of it as the pain pulsated through it. He tried to open his eyes, but the excruciating pain prevented that. He moved his head a bit more and the pain once again drove him into darkness. He didn't see where he was lying, or the scattered debris around him. A rustling under dead leaves against one wall didn't rouse him, as two beady eyes peeked out before a small brown field mouse scampered across, stopping to watch the large form laying motionless. Nose twitching, the mouse continued on its way.

The leader of the men who had captured him stood over him. How was he to be used if he couldn't wake up? They had no one else, just him. He turned to the door, slamming it behind him and motioning for it to be locked. He stood, staring at the three men gathered near him, then giving new orders, sent them on their way.

Chapter 19

Dave and his partner, Tom, watched the street numbers as they sped down the road.

"It should be along in here, on your side, Tom." Dave slowed the ambulance he was driving. "There."

"I don't see anyone, do you?"

Dave shook his head. "No, I don't. They may be inside with the victim."

"I don't know, Dave. Something just doesn't feel right."

"I have that feeling too, Tom, but we have to answer this call. We can't refuse." Dave slowed the ambulance and came to a stop as a man rushed towards him.

"Back here. I don't know if it's a heart attack or not. He just dropped. I've tried CPR but he's not responding."

Dave followed the man as Tom ran for the back of the ambulance and their gear. Time would be of the essence if it was a heart attack.

Dave dropped to his knees beside the man lying prone on the ground. As he reached for the man's wrist to feel for a pulse, he felt something hard jam into his back. He stopped moving. What was going on? Tom had been right. There was something wrong with this. He felt movement in front of him. The victim was no longer laying flat and still but was rising to his feet, pulling a mask over his head before he turned around. Dave's hands raised, he was not sure exactly what was going on.

Dave was yanked to his feet and pushed back the way he had come. Tom was standing near at the front of the ambulance, a weapon pointed at him. Their eyes met. What did these guys want? Neither one of them had been in this kind of situation. Dave had receive his training in the armed forces and served a tour overseas but even that not prepared him for an attack on his own ground.

Dave was shoved to the back of the ambulance.

"What do you want?" he demanded. "We don't carry narcotics."

"We need you to come with us."

Dave shook his head. "Not happening. We go nowhere." He couldn't duck the hand that came up, striking him across the face and sending him into the open vehicle door. He struggled to rebalance himself on his feet, hand going to his mouth. He tasted the blood from the split lip.

"Get what you need."

Again, he was shoved forward and into the ambulance. "What am I treating?" On pretence of feeling the shoulder that had rammed into the door, he flicked his radio to the send position.

"Someone with a head injury."

"A head injury? You've got to be kidding me. That person needs to be in a hospital. I'm a paramedic, not a physician." He stared into the weapon that was pointed at his heart.

"You will get what you need and come with us. Or you and your partner both die today and we find someone else."

Dave could only hope his radio was sending the conversation to dispatch and they would send them help. He tried to think of everything he would need, pulling out equipment boxes and supplies.

"Is he having trouble breathing?" They stared at him. "I need to know if he's having trouble breathing, the person you want me to see. If he does, you'll need oxygen."

"It doesn't matter. We just need to you wake him up long enough for him to tell us something."

Dave shook his head at them. "It doesn't work that way with head injuries. It could take days or weeks for that person to rouse, if he even does." Dave's eyes sought for Tom out of the front window, but couldn't see him. "Where's my partner?"

"He's safe for now, as long as you do what we say."

Dave sighed, knowing he had no choice. As he pulled the last box he had chosen from the ambulance, he was stopped, and the radio was ripped from his body and stomped on.

The men with him grabbed the boxes and motioned him forward. He walked towards the van that had parked behind the ambulance and stopped. The equipment was loaded and then Dave was shoved forward once again, this time catching his legs on the edge of the van and barely keeping his balance. His hands were roughly tied behind him and a blindfold was tightened around his face before he was shoved inside and to the floor. He heard the door slam and then the vehicle moved backwards. He heard the familiar sound of the ambulance motor and his heart sank. Where was Tom?

He could hear the sirens of approaching cruisers but knew it was too late for him. He prayed that Tom was alive and they could find him.

The cruisers slammed to a stop at the address. The officers couldn't see the ambulance, but could tell a heavy vehicle had been there. They cautiously made their way down the lane and to the house, puzzled at not finding anyone.

Frankie watched as the men and women scoured the area. This just didn't make sense. It was Dave's unit and Dave would never have left without letting them know. He had heard the portion of the call that Dave had been able to get through. He turned and searched the area around. Where are you, Dave? He turned as an officer approached him and handed him an evidence bag.

"Is this Dave's?"   He looked at the crushed radio in his hand.

"We're not sure, but it was found near where we think the ambulance was parked. There's not a lot to go on, Frankie."

"I know."   He stopped as he heard the tones over his radio and then the address given. "I'm heading over there. Sounds like they found the ambulance."

"Hope they found Dave and Tom as well."

Frankie parked in the area behind the old rundown school house. The ambulance was out of place. It shouldn't be here. He walked towards the office who had found it.

"Any sign of the paramedics."

"Not in the cab. I was waiting for backup before I opened the back."

"Let me have your pry bar, then, and we'll get it opened."

A few seconds' work, and Frankie had the door open. Tom lay inside, not moving. Please, Lord, Frankie breathed, let him be alive. He was up in the back and bending over him, finding a pulse.

"He's alive. Let's get some help for him."

Frankie stared around, then his eyes stopped. Equipment boxes were gone. He had stood at the back of an ambulance enough times to know what should or shouldn't be there.

Caleb tracked him down outside Tom's door in the hospital. "How is he?"

"He's awake and fighting mad. It doesn't make sense what he's saying. He says Dave had gone ahead to assess the patient, then in a couple of minutes returned with the men, gun to his back. Tom had been held with a gun to his head. He couldn't heard the conversation or see what was going on with Dave at the back of the ambulance. He did hear some raised voices at one point before he was knocked out."

"Can he give a description?"

"Other than height, weight and clothing, and that he heard a van, no. They were masked and wore gloves."

"Of course they did. Why wouldn't they?" Caleb was frustrated. He had a dead suspect, Abe had a missing team member, they still had a woman in danger, and now they had a paramedic assaulted with his partner missing. "I'm heading back to the office, to see what's come in. Let me know if something turns up."

"I will."

Chapter 20

Dave felt the van slow and turn, moving even slower until it stopped. He waited knowing he wouldn't have a chance to get away. He was pulled from the van and with a weapon to his back directed forward, a hand on his arm helping him to stay upright. He heard the rasp of a lock being opened, the squeak of rusty hinges, then he was pushed through, stumbling and dropping awkwardly to his knees. Sounds came behind him and then his hands were freed. He pushed to his feet, rubbing at his wrists and turned.

"Keep the blindfold on," he was ordered. "We'll be back in a while."

"And just where is here?" Dave didn't see the hand that was raised but once again felt the blow across his face, knocking him to his hands and knees. He shook his head to clear it vaguely hearing the door lock. Well, Lord, it looks like it's just You and me. You didn't have to go to these lengths to get my attention.

He turned his body so he could sit, one leg tucked almost under him, the other raised and bent at the knee. Arm on his knee, he rested his head down to catch his breath. He finally raised both hands to undo the blindfold, dropping it to the ground in front of him. He turned slowly, studying the building he was locked into: old, he thought, but solid. Not a lot of places to get through to get out. Then his eyes dropped to the ground in front of him and the body lying there.

Dropping to his knees, he reached by habit to check for a pulse. It was there, weak but the man was still alive. He felt along the limbs and torso for injuries and felt none, then turned his attention to the wound on the man's head. He sat back on his heels. Who was this? He turned the man carefully onto his back. Murphy! It was Murphy he had been brought to tend to, and he knew that neither one would make it out alive, not unless somehow they were found.

He spun and looked. Yes, his equipment and supply boxes had been brought in. First things first, he thought. Reaching for the stethoscope in his uniform cargo pants pocket, he turned back to Murphy, listening to the heart and lungs. So far, he seemed okay, but Dave was worried. It was cold and damp in here and he had no idea how long Murphy had been there.

He then turned his attention to the head wound. What did they hit you with, Murphy, he thought as he reached to clean it and then bandage it. It had been a brutal blow and it looked as if Murphy had been moving towards his assailant at the time.

Dave finally sat back on his heels. Murphy needed an IV and how was he to hang it where he was lying? It would mean moving him and he didn't like that idea.

He rose and searched the building, finally finding a place where a nail head protruded enough to hold the IV bag, but it meant moving Murphy. He didn't have a choice.

Murphy settled where he wanted him, Dave reached to start the IV, hanging the bag just as the lock opened behind him. He stood and turned. The leader stood there, mask in place.

"Has he awakened yet?"

Dave shook his head. "No and he may not. It was a very brutal blow, and he may well have a skull fracture."

"Wake him up!"

Dave stared at him in disbelief. "I just told you, he may have a skull fracture. I can't just wake him up. It doesn't work that way. He could have bleeding on the brain, brain swelling, brain damage."

"Wake him up. I want him awake when I next return."

"Didn't you just hear me? He may never awaken. I"m not a doctor, certainly not a neurosurgeon, but I know you can't expect head injury patients just to wake up. And in this damp cold building, he's like to develop pneumonia."

Dave watched as the man walked away, the door locking behind him. Shaking his head, he turned back to Murphy, dropping down beside him to reassess him. Lord, he needs the hospital. Even overseas, I had better access to health care for my men. Hearing rustling, he turned slowly, searching the dimness for the noise. Then he smiled. The little mouse had once more made its appearance, stopping to watch him, whiskers twitching, then scampering away. Dave thoughtfully studied the walls, turned back to Murphy, then rose to once more walk through the room. If there was a way out, he was determined to find it and get both himself and Murphy away. Where was the mouse getting in and out?

Eddie turned as he heard his name called. Frankie was walking rapidly towards him, sheaf of papers in hand.

"We have surveillance tape from near where the ambulance was dropped off. We've picked up a van coming away from that area. I'm having the plates run now."

"You realize it was probably stolen and already dumped."

"I know but I can always hope. Tom hasn't been able to add much more. The voice on the transmission with Dave's isn't clear, so we're not getting a lot from it."

"No, it would be too easy, now wouldn't it?" Eddie was frustrated. He felt like all they are doing was running into dead ends. "Come find me if you get anything else."

Joseph watched as Adriel stood at the front window, staring out, a defeated droop to her shoulders. They had come up with nothing in their search. It was like Murphy had vanished into thin air. Abe stopped beside him, then motioned him back to the kitchen, pouring coffee from the never-ending pot.

"I just got off the phone with Frankie." Abe sank wearily down into a chair.

"It doesn't sound as if it was good news."

"I don't think it is, though it may be in the long run. Dave and his partner were ambushed on a run today, a set up. Dave's disappeared, and his partner's in the hospital with a head injury. They think Dave was taken to look after Murphy."

Joseph nodded. "That would make sense. The only way to take Murphy down would be with a gun butt or an iron fist, and if that's the case, then they would need someone to look after him and his head injury." He gestured with his chin towards the living room. "You'll have to tell her, you know. She'll find out somehow."

Abe sighed. "I know I will and I don't want to get her expectations up. We don't know any of this for sure."

"What don't you want to tell me, Abe?" Adriel was standing behind him. Neither man had heard her come into the kitchen.

Abe pushed back the chair beside him with his foot. She sat, still staring at him. He looked away from her, then back. "You know Dave from town, the paramedic?" At her nod, he stated, "He and his partner were ambushed today on a fake call, and Dave is missing. There's speculation he was taken to look after Murphy. We don't have any evidence to support that."

She nodded.   "Yes, I can see that. Murphy's tough, and you're not getting him down without hurting him. It's the same for all of you. So where do we go from here?"

"We keep looking for Murphy, now Dave, and we work on keeping you safe."   Abe watched the flicker of emotions cross her face. "And no, you're not going to the media, or offering to trade yourself for him. Murphy would be adamant that doesn't happen, and you need to listen to us who know him best."

She nodded, then rose. "Let me know what you find out about Dave."

Joseph watched her walk away. "That was too easy, Abe. Something's up with her."

"I know. I'll have Rebecca talk to her. Maybe she can find out."

Chapter 21

Dave bent over Murphy again. It was getting dark and he had no other light than what came through the windows. Murphy had not moved at all since Dave had gotten him situated near the wall. Hearing the lock on the door, Dave stood and walked to the middle of the building, facing the door.

A light proceeded the men into the room, blinding Dave.

"Is he awake?"

Dave shook his head. "I told you. He won't wake up just because you want him to. Whoever hit him, they hit him too hard. He may never awaken. Besides that, I need some light and I need some way to keep him warm. If he isn't kept warm, he'll get sicker and then there'll never be a chance he'll awaken."

The leader turned and spoke quietly to one of the men who left. "You had better be speaking the truth, or you will die too."

"The way I figure it, I'm not making it out of here alive anyway, nor is Murphy. So what does it matter what I say?"

Dave picked himself up gingerly from the dirt where he had been knocked, tasting blood once again on his mouth. His hand went to his ribs, cradling them as he arose. He needed to stop provoking this guy, but the words just kept coming. He watched as a battery operated lantern and blankets were brought in and dropped on the floor as well as food and water.

"Here. The next time, he had better be awake."

"Go take a medical course and learn about head injuries. Then, next time, maybe your guys won't hit as hard." Dave walked away from them and back to Murphy, not caring if they attacked him again or not. His main concern was his friend.

He picked up the lantern and turned it on, not hearing the door shut and lock behind him. He reached for his stethoscope again. He was getting worried. Murphy's lungs weren't sounding as clear as they should. Pneumonia was likely setting in, given his surroundings and his inability to move around.

He reached for the blankets and tucked one under Murphy, and then spread two of the over him. He kept the thinnest one for himself. Raising Murphy's head slightly, he managed to get him to swallow a little of the water. He reached for a bottle for himself and drank, eyes glued to Murphy. He turned at a thought, then rose and went towards the door. It opened under his hand. He closed the door again, not sure if it was just an oversight or a trap. If it was a trap, he wasn't falling for it. And if he tried to get the out of there in the dark, the reflective tape sewn on his clothing would be a dead giveaway.

Abe tracked Rebecca down in the cabin she and Gideon had chosen and then remodelled for their own.

"Rebecca, if you have some time, can you talk to Adriel?"

"Sure, I can, but why?"

"Joseph picked up something with her today, but isn't quite sure what. I told him I'd get you to talk to her."

Rebecca sat back from the photos she had been studying, trying to pick out the ones she needed for a friend. "I can tell you what part of it is. She's really missing Murphy and really worried about him. I also think she's not feeling well. She hasn't eaten well or slept much in the last month. I can't get her to do either. The best sleep she's had in a while is when we got that sleeping pill down her, and she won't take any more."

Abe sighed. "I thought it was something like that. I talked to Caleb. They have no idea where Murphy is, and now Dave's gone missing."

"Dave? Missing? When did this happen?"

"You hadn't heard? Earlier today. Tom's in the hospital. The speculation is that Dave was taken to care for Murphy."

"I pray he was and that means Murphy is still alive, at least for now."

Adriel sank down onto her bed. She was tired, so tired in fact that she could barely think straight, let alone walk straight. Lord, she prayed, let me sleep tonight. I don't want to take any medication if I can help it and I know that this is where's it headed to. She turned and as she turned, the room swirled around her. She collapsed, landing on the floor in a heap.

Rebecca tapped at her door, then not getting an answer, opened it. She yelled for Abe to go get Matt, then dropped to her knees by her friend. She could feel the heat from her body as she reached to touch her. Adriel had a high fever. No wonder Joseph thought something was wrong. She heard Matt beside her, then he was bending over Adriel.

"Rebecca, turn down the bed clothes. I need to get her up there. Has she mentioned not feeling well?"

Rebecca shook her head. "No, she hasn't. I thought she hadn't been, but I've been so busy I haven't checked with her and I know Sarah and Elizabeth haven't either."

"It's not your fault. Let me get my gear and I'll check her out. Can you get her into something that easier to take care of her?"

Rebecca nodded, then searched for other clothing for Adriel. T-shirt, she thought, shorts, or pyjama pants. That would work. By the time Matt was tapping at the door again, she had Adriel settled back into bed, just a sheet over her, and cold cloths on her head.

"Good. This should be fine." Matt went to work, listening to her heart, her breathing, taking her pulse. "Does she have any allergies that you know of? Any recent bites?"

Rebecca shook her head, tears near the surface. "She's so private, Matt, she doesn't give out a lot of information about herself."

"That's okay, Rebecca. We'll figure it out. I called Paul Woods at the clinic down town. He's on his way."

"Good." Rebecca looked behind her to see Gideon standing here. "Gideon, has Murphy said anything about any health issues with Adriel?"

"No, he hasn't, other than that incident when she was poisoned. He never felt that she was completely over it. I just wanted to let you know, Matt, that Paul's here and on his way in."

Paul stood in the kitchen, facing Abe and Gideon. Matt and Rebecca were still with Adriel.

"She's really sick, Abe. I wish I could move her to the hospital, but it's not the best place for her. From what I understand, she was poisoned a while ago?"

"She was. I don't know if they totally narrowed it down to a single chemical or food." Abe watched Paul's face. "What are you saying?"

"I'm saying that she never got over it totally, that the stress with Murphy disappearing has triggered something laying dormant and made it flare again." He looked at each one of them. "We've a fight on our hands. I've been in touch with the nurses I know who do private duty. Two of them will be out in the morning, each taking 12 hour shifts. I trust them implicitly. They know what's up and will take every effort to help you keep her safe. I've also arranged for oxygen to be delivered. Do you have any idea at all where Murphy is?" At the negative movement of Abe's head, he sighed. "Somehow, I thought that would be your answer. He's the key to getting her better."

Abe nodded. "Do what you need to for her, Paul. Whatever we can bring in, or whoever we need to, we will. We'll work the security aspects out. We just need to find Murphy." Abe turned and walked away at that point, deep in thought, trying to figure out who had taken Murphy. He needed to talk to Caleb, if not him, then Eddie or Frankie. One of them needed to know what was happening.

Chapter 22

Abe finally tracked Caleb down the next morning. Caleb took one look at him, then pointed out the door. Once seated at a booth in Mac's, Caleb turned to Abe.

"What's wrong, Abe? I can tell something is."

Abe sighed, then spoke. "Adriel collapsed last night. Matt called in Paul Woods. He thinks it's some residual from her poisoning and that Murphy's disappearance triggered it. Rebecca said she hasn't been eating or sleeping like she should. Joseph picked up on something yesterday. Paul's arranged for special duty nurses for us round the clock."

"That's not good." Caleb picked up his cup of tea. "We haven't had any contact from the kidnappers about either Murphy and now we figure Dave."

"Murphy must be bad if what you suspect is right and Dave was kidnapped to care for him."

Caleb nodded. "We haven't had a word, and that worries me. We should have had something by now." He stopped as his phone dinged a text message. He read it, then passed his phone to Abe.

Abe shot a look at Caleb. "That's Dave, not Murphy."

"I know. So where is Murphy? Dave looks a little battered. Knowing him, he's probably said something he shouldn't have."

"That note really doesn't give us a lot, and them wanting to talk to Adriel, that won't be happening now, either. What do we do, Caleb?"

"We ask to speak with Murphy first, or to see that he is still alive." Caleb sat back as Mac set their food in front of them and then walked away. Caleb contemplated what was in front of him, not really hungry, but knowing he needed to eat.

"Have you any leads at all?"

Caleb shook his head, then looked up at someone paused at the window. He excused himself and went to meet the woman who had motioned for him. Abe idly watched, then stared more intently at the woman. She reminded him of someone, but with the tattered jeans, faded T-shirt and battered baseball hat, he couldn't place who it was.

Caleb slid back into his seat and set the envelope down.

"That was Tracker. She said Jace had come through with some information for us and she volunteered to bring it in. She was told to find me here."

"That's Tracker?"

Caleb nodded. "You've never met her."

"No, but she reminds me of someone. But then by now, everyone does."

Caleb leafed through the material once he was back in his office. Tracker was right. Jace had come through.   He stood to go and find Frankie or Eddie, then paused. It was interesting that Abe thought she reminded him of someone. He didn't think he had ever heard Abe mention that about a woman.   He sat back down, pondering that, then raised his heart to the Lord for all his friends he was seeking to help right now. It was only the Lord who could heal and protect them, and lead the investigators to where they were.

"Frankie, can you find Eddie? Jace has come through."   Caleb had tracked Frankie down in his office.

Frankie looks up from his paperwork. "He has? We'll meet you in your office?"

"Conference room. We're going to need to spread it out and then start having it matched to what we have."   Caleb turned to leave, then pulled out his phone. "I've sent a text message I received off to the lab."

Frankie studied it. "The same ones who have Murphy?"

"That's my thought. We wait for them to contact us again. The only thing is, I just saw Abe. Adriel collapsed last night."

Frankie had started to rise, then sat back down. "Now that really doesn't help, does it?"

"No, it doesn't. They're wanting to speak with her. When they contact us again, we ask for Murphy and no one else."

"I hope we can get away with that. I'll let you know what I find out from any of this."

Abe turned as Rebecca entered the kitchen. "Abe, I know Paul trusts those women, but I don't. I think we need to get them out of here on some pretext."

"What makes you say that?"

"The questions they're asking. They're asking questions about the set up here, how we work. It's more than just a concern for their own safety."

They both turned as they heard Matt's raised voice, something they seldom heard from him. Running to Adriel's bedroom, they found Matt standing in front of the bed, in an attitude of protection.

"Matt, what's wrong?"

"Wrong? I caught her trying to give Adriel an injection that wasn't authorized. Rebecca, check her pockets. Go on, do it."

Rebecca hesitated, then moved to do what Matt had asked. She pulled a vial out and read the label aloud, her face paling as she did so.

"This kills, doesn't it?"

"It does. And with Adriel down like she it, it wouldn't take much."

Abe reached for the vial in his sister's hand. "Go, call Caleb, and then find the other nurse and bring her here. Then find Ian and Joseph. Once you've done that, go and stay with Gideon." Abe's eyes had never moved from the nurse, who remained defiant in her stance.

Rebecca ran to do what her brother had requested. Ian stood beside Matt, a strong barrier to Adriel. Then as Matt turned to monitor her, he moved to stand between Matt and the nurse still facing the bed. The other nurse had been seated in a chair just outside the room, fear in her face, Joseph on guard beside her.

Abe went to meet Caleb outside the house. Caleb was shocked, then nodded.

"Someone doesn't want her to talk. How far has this gone?"

"I don't know. I know Paul said he trusts these two women completely, but obviously we can't. I want both of them out of here. I've removed Paul from being the doctor. He understands but doesn't like it. I have a call in to John Thompson, from the church. He's on his way out. His wife's a nurse and he's bringing her."

"We've had no further word from the kidnappers since the text this morning. They'll be waiting for a response, but we don't respond until they send another text. It's tough waiting, I know, Abe, but it's standard. At this point, with them using Dave as the messenger, we can't be sure Murphy still alive or even if he is in any condition to talk to us.”

Abe nodded. “I understand. Now, let’s get you in to speak with that nurse. Both of them are to be gone when you leave.”

Matt turned to John Thompson. “We’ve had a fight on our hands, John. Her fever’s down some but still higher than it should be.”

John was doing own assessment, his wife moving in tandem with him, having worked with him enough to anticipate his moves.

“Lungs are clear. Heart sounds okay. Was any blood drawn?”

“Paul had blood drawn last night, but I’m not sure if it even got to the lab. We’ll draw more, I take it?”

John nodded as his wife, Ruth, moved to draw the blood and label it with Adriel’s information. “I’ll call ahead to the lab if you can have someone take it.”

“Joseph volunteered to.” He handed the package to Joseph.

“I’ve put a rush on it and the lab knows that. They’ll get the results to us as soon as they can.” John stood back, assessed Adriel. “I remember how sick she was and how she recovered. She shouldn’t have had a relapse. All her labs were clear. There is no way, as Paul claimed, there should have been any residue left. It wouldn’t come back this way.” He turned to Matt. “Talk to me, Matt. Tell me about how she's been acting, eating, whatever you can think of. Ruth, check for medicines, toothpastes. You know what I want."

He listened as Matt described what he and the others had noted over the last couple of weeks. He turned as Ruth came up to him, a vitamin bottle in her hand.

"I found this, John. What's inside is not what she thought she was taking. Something was switched on her."

John's eyes sought his wife's and then he nodded. He poured out some of the tablets, then wetting his finger, rubbed one and tasted his finger. He spat out what he had tasted.

"I've found our source of poison from before. Thanks, Ruth." He turned to Matt. "Can you get this to the lab? This is what has been making her sick. And if I give you a script for medication, will you stop at the hospital and get it filled for me? On second thought, I'll call it in and all you'll have to do is pick it up Can Joseph do that while he's there?"

Matt nodded. "I'll make sure he does.

Chapter 23

Caleb wasn't supposed to be in the office that late, but a conference call he had been expecting had been late starting. He looked up as Matt appeared in his door, a bag in his hand.

"What do you have there, Matt?"

"Poison, John tells me."

"Poison?"

Matt nodded. "John had his wife go through everything Adriel had in her medicine cabinet. She found this and John says it's likely what caused her poisoning in the first place. She got better in hospital because she wasn't taking them, but then started getting sick again when she was home and back on them. He's figured out the antidote and Joseph's picking it up when he takes in the blood work to the hospital."

"All along, it was there. How did our lab miss that?"

Matt shrugged. "I have no idea. I would like to know how she got them in the first place." He paused, already knowing the answer before he asked. "Any word on Murphy or Dave?"

Caleb shook his head. "Nothing. I just pray that they're together and both are alive."

Caleb watched Matt walk again, defeat in his demeanour. Lord, we need a miracle here. Any time would be nice.

Abe watched as John and Matt stood talking in the kitchen. He couldn't hear their words but this sternness on their faces worried him. He moved closer as John turned.

"Abe, just who I wanted to see. Matt's talked with Caleb and they can't figure out how the lab team missed the vitamins."

"From my recollection, it wasn't a crime scene tech who went to her house, just an officer, and he was asked to bring food and beverage and cleaning supplies. If he wasn't told to bring from the medicine cabinet, then he not likely thought of that."

"That makes sense. She's turned a corner now, I think, Abe. I was telling Matt Ruth has her resting comfortably and asleep on her own. I'll run a day or so of treatment in her IV and then repeat the blood work at that point."

"That's good news. We could use some." Abe turned to walk away, then turned back. "How sure are you that the vitamins are the cause?"

"What do you mean, Abe?"

"I mean, I've never heard her talking about taking any vitamins. Rebecca's mentioned that Adriel favours travel-sized sets of shampoos, toothpaste, that kind of stuff, gets rid of it every three weeks or so, and buys fresh. So if it's not in her food, she doesn't take vitamins, replaces her personal care products routinely, how was she poisoned first and then again?"

John stared at him. "That's a good point. I think we all assumed it was something like that, as it usually is. I'll need to rethink how it could be introduced to her."

"What does she use on a regular basis: key, phone, pen? It would need to be something she carries with her."

"You're right. We'll need to go through her purse and her other belongings. I can get Ruth to go through her clothing and see if there's something in there we should be looking at. I'll have her bring you Adriel's purse."

Matt and Abe exchanged glances as they watched John walk back to the bedroom.

"Do you really think it's something different?"

Abe nodded. "I do. Go stop John from going through her belongings. We need a police presence for that, to make it legal in court."

Abe watched as Frankie carefully pulled all the items from Adriel's purse.

"She really doesn't carry a lot in her purse, does she?" Frankie commented as he searched through what she had. "Abe, you can verify what I'm looking at. First, her wallet."

Frankie looked through her wallet, naming what he found. Then he turned to the rest.

"She doesn't have any medication, no lip stuff the ladies like, no perfume."

"The only other things are the pen and pencil she has."

Frankie picked up the pen and studied it, holding it closer. "There, we have it. I see just a faint residue on the end. The same for the pencil, where she would twist it. Someone got to these." He sealed the pen and pencil into evidence bags, then replaced all the items in Adriel's purse. "Let her know we had to go through it."

Abe took the proffered purse and set it aside to return to her room. "I will. She won't be happy."

"Better unhappy than dead. Now I have to go figure out how the drug or poison got on them."

"I would say it's something recent but you'll know better once you get the lab report back."

Frankie nodded. "We still have to figure out who and this just complicates things if it's someone different, and I think it was."

Abe turned as Ruth entered the room. "How is she now, Ruth?"

"Sleeping naturally, I'd say. John found the right combination of medications to use, even without knowing fully what the poison was. God led there, I would say." She looked down as she felt something brush her leg. "Oh, what a beautiful dog!"

"That's Adriel's dog, Echo." Abe replied.

"Then why is she out here and not in with Adriel?"

Abe stared at her. "You mean, you'll let her in? The other nurses absolutely refused."

"They both need each other. Echo, go find Adriel. Go on, girl," Ruth repeated. Echo took one last look and ran down the hall to find Adriel and was up on the bed and snuggled down tight to her mistress before they could say she couldn't.

Frankie shook his head as he left. What next?

Abe stood at his office window, staring at nothing. Where is Murphy, Lord? Our team's not complete without him.

Dave roused from his light slumber and gazed around through bleary eyes, blinking to bring them into focus. No, it wasn't some nightmare, it was reality that he was involved in. He turned to Murphy to assess him. It was still dark, early morning he figured.

Murphy was stirring finally, Dave noted, eyes flickering open and closed, finally opening but not focusing.

"Murphy?" Dave's voice was quiet. He couldn't be sure if someone was outside the building or not.

Murphy blinked, bringing his eyes to Dave. "Dave? Where are we?"

"Somewhere out in the boonies, Murphy. You were kidnapped from your compound. They brought me out to treat you. How's your head?"

"It hurts, but not as much as it did. I think I've been awake on and off for the last couple of days."

"That sounds right." Dave reached to pull the IV. "I had you on an IV. We need to be very cautious. I've told them you may never awaken. Play along with me."

"Gladly. Now, how do we get out of here?"

"That I'm not sure of. You're not strong enough to walk yet, and the leader keeps coming back to see if you're alert. He's desperate to use you to get to Adriel, is what I figured."

Murphy started to nod, then stopped. "That's what I figure. The last I remember is Ian telling us we had been breached and heading out. Is Adriel okay?"

"I hadn't heard what happened, but I would assume so if they want you awake so bad." Dave turned as he heard a noise. "Stay quiet, and keep your eyes closed. We need a few more hours to get you back on your feet."

Dave moved away from Murphy to stand by the window. The door opened and there was silence. He heard someone enter and just stand watching. He finally turned. It was a stranger.

"Dave, come with me. Here, I'll help you with your friend."

Dave walked towards the man. "Jason?" His voice was low. "What are you doing here?"

"You know me, I like the outdoors. I was camping over by the next ridge and saw the smoke from here. No one should be in this place right now, so I came to check. Your guards aren't very good. They're all in the cabin. If we move quickly enough, we'll get away."

Dave turned to Murphy, who was watching intently. "Murphy, this is a good friend. God's provided for us again. He'll get us out of here. He knows the woods around here like no one else."

Jason helped Dave get Murphy to his feet, steadying him as Dave gathered up what supplies he thought he would need and that he could stuff in his pockets. Cautiously, they made their way slowly out of the building and around back, disappearing into the blackness of the night. A whisper of movement in the building, and a little black nose followed by whiskers and beady eyes showed. Then the little mouse scampered towards the food that was left. A banquet, it must have thought.

Jason silently pointed to where he had left his camp. Looking behind him, he listened, then nodded. So far, so good. If he could get the two men to his camp, then he could get them out to safety.

Dave paused for a minute, to give Murphy a chance to rest. "Doing okay, Murphy?"

Murphy nodded, a painful movement to his head. "I'll get there. I know we need to keep going. Thanks for stopping for a minute, Murphy."

"How much farther, Jason?"

"About a mile. We'll make it. I doubt they'll be around until morning. I was watching for a night or two, trying to figure out what they were up to. I got in close enough to hear them and knew I had to get in there to get to you two. They're really stupid, you know."

Dave gave a low laugh. "I know. They didn't lock the door behind them, did they?"

Jason shook his head in disgust. "No, they didn't. And they didn't post any guards outside. What kind of group are they with?"

Dave shrugged. "I have no idea. I was nabbed to come look after Murphy here."

"Murphy?" Jason turned to peer at him. "Nope, never met you before." Then he turned and headed off.

"Are you sure you can trust him, Dave?" Murphy's voice was low enough Dave barely caught his words.

"We can. He had my back many times overseas. We were in the same unit."

Jason stopped at the cabin he had been using. He pointed at his jeep. "You two get in. I'll be about five minutes, if that."

True to his word, Jason was back in less than five minutes, stuffing a duffle bag into the bag and then climbing behind the wheel. He peered through the darkness, seeing nothing that alarmed him.

He turned in his seat to look at Dave in the back seat. "Where to?"

Dave and Murphy exchanged a glance. "We need to get Murphy assessed by a doctor, but I'm not keen on an Emergency room."

Jason nodded. "I know who. Trust me."

Murphy shot him a look, then laid his head back on the headrest. It was really starting to pound and he refused to ask for any pain medications.

Dave watched Murphy, assessing him. He knew the minute Murphy lost consciousness again.

"Jason, where are we heading?"

"There's a doctor that goes to your church, right?"

Dave nodded. "John Thompson. What about him?"

"He works in Emergency, doesn't he? Then let's get your friend to him."

"How do you know John?"

"We've talked a few times. I've been at your church. Sitting way up in the balcony. John's sat with me when I'm there."

"That's John. Okay, let's get Murphy to him. Do you have a phone?"

Jason pulled his phone out and tossed it back to Dave. "Just be careful who you call. The people over here are crazy and scary."

"Tell me about it, Jason." He paused, looking at the phone. Who could he call? Finally, he punched in a number.

"John? It's Dave Allison."

"Dave! Where are you?"

"Right now I'm with a friend. We have Murphy, but he's been hurt. I need to get to you to have you assess him." Dave went on to describe the injury.

"If they know you've gotten away, they'll be watching Abe's." Silence came through the line. "Have your friend bring you here. We're back far enough from the road so it should be okay. When you get close to the house, have your friends flick his lights on and off. Then he can pull right into our garage. Dave, I'm glad you two are safe."

John thoughtfully closed his phone. Thank you, Lord, they're safe. Now to keep them that way. He needed to call someone, but which one? Ruth. It wouldn't be strange if he called his wife, now would it?

Ruth answered her phone, then turned to look at Abe as she talked. Moving towards him, she laid her hand on his arm to keep him from moving away. Positioning her phone so Abe could hear too, she continued her conversation.

"Okay, John. Abe's here in the room. What was the message you wanted me to pass on?"

"Can you let me know I have his packages safe? I'll bring them out next time I come, if I can remember. You know what's my memory's like at time, Ruth."

"That I do, John. Stay safe."

She pocketed her phone, and looked up to Find Abe's intent stare on her face.

"Packages, Ruth?   I don't have any packages that John would need to pick up."

She smiled, tilted her head and then shook it. "Oh, I think you do. Two in fact." She watched as he tried to work it through, then shook his head.

"I'm sorry, Ruth. I'm not following you." As she continued to watch his face, she saw the dawning comprehension.   "He has my two packages. Oh, that's wonderful." He reached out to hug Ruth. "Thank you, Ruth. He'll let you know how much they were damaged in shipment, won't he?"

"I'm sure he will. Now, go. You've got men waiting for orders. Scat."

Abe laughed as he turned from her and headed for the door. Yes, Murphy and Dave were safe. John would get them to him when he could. He pulled out his phone. He needed to reach Caleb.

"Caleb?   Abe.   John Thompson just called. He has a couple of packages for me."

"Packages?   Oh, I see what you mean. Good. Let me know when you have them."

"That I will. He's taking care of them for us."

Abe pushed the door open to the gym, knowing the team members had gathered there

to work off their frustrations. He stood and
watched for a minute, then spoke rapidly. The
team spread out to take on their tasks.

Dave stood and watched as John assessed Murphy's head wound. Murphy had not roused when they reached the Thompsons and had been carried into John's home office.

"How is he, John?" Dave's voice was quiet.

"I don't think there's any fracture. And you said he was alert and knew you. That's good. I would say a concussion. I'm glad you were with him. That likely kept him alive. He wouldn't have survived long being dehydrated."

John stood, then shook his head "I don't understand, Dave. How did they know to grab you and not someone else?"

Dave's eyes were on Murphy, then raised to John. "That's what I want to know. Someone's been watching us closely, I would say. Now to Murphy. Do we need to get him to Emerge?"

John shook his head. "Not right away. If he keeps losing consciousness or other symptoms develop, I would say yes. But for now, let's leave him here. We can hear from the kitchen. Jason, come on. Let's get some food into you two."

Dave took one last look at Murphy, then followed John. "Where's Ruth?"

John spun, surprise on his face. "That's right. You don't know." He proceeded to explain what had happened and why Ruth wasn't there.

"Poisoned? By who?" Dave was puzzled.

John shook his head. "We don't know that yet."

"That lady on the board that doesn't like her." Jason's voice broke into the conversation. "Try her."

The two other men spun to face him. "How do you know that?"

"I didn't until now. But I've heard her talking when she's out and about. She's very careless with her words. She was looking for someone to plant poison on someone, but I didn't know who. She was very careful that she didn't say anything that would incriminate her."

"And you recognized her?"

"Of course. Someone who treats you like the scum of the earth is always remembered." Jason moved towards the fridge. "Do you mind, John?"

"No, help yourself. I'm not sure what all you'll find. Try the freezer too. Ruth usually has meals prepared and frozen."

John watched as Jason rummaged in the fridge and freezer. Dave had turned back to the office, trying to decide who he should call. John stopped in the doorway.

"Who do you want to call, Dave? We have to tell someone."

Dave nodded, eyes staring at the forested landscape painting over the fireplace. "I don't know, John. Caleb, Eddie, Frankie. Take your pick." He turned. "You call. You heard him just as plainly as I did. I would like to stay off the radar as much as I can."

The sound of the doorbell, startled both of them. John motioned Dave to stay and pulled the door closed. Jason was a common enough visitor to his home that he wasn't worried about him. He picked out the side window, then pulled the door open.

"Matt, what brings you by? Did Ruth send you after something she needed?"

"She did, I think. She found me, handed me this note, and told me I had to come now." Matt's face didn't give away that it was a ploy to get one of Abe's men into the house.

"Come in. Here, let me see what Ruth wanted." He turned to head for the kitchen. "Oh, by the way, that painting you talked about seeing? It's in the office. Go on in. I'll be there in a minute. I'll just tell Jason we have another guest for a meal."

"Thanks, John. Food sounds good." Matt hesitated before he opened the door, not sure what he would find on the other side.

The dim light didn't give much away. He sent movement to his side and ducked.

"Dave or Murphy? Which one is that?"

"Matt?" Dave's voice came from behind him as the lights came on. "Sorry, I wasn't sure who it was, just that it wasn't John."

"You okay?" At Dave's nod, Matt turned. "Murphy?" He moved towards the couch where his team mate lay.

"Concussion. Dehyration. I did what I could for him with what I had."

"We know you did, Dave. Just asking how he is."

"John says he should be okay. How's Adriel?"

"She's better now that we know how she was poisoned and John could administer the antidote. We could have lost her."

Matt turned back to stare at Dave. "How'd you get away?"

"God. The door was left unlocked. My buddy Jason just happened to be up there camping, and came to find out what was going on where nothing should have been going on. He walked in and walked out with us."

Matt shook his head. "Sounds unbelievable, but you're standing here. Abe was glad to hear you're both safe."

John stood in the doorway. "We have food ready. Come and eat while we make plans."

"We need to get in touch with Caleb. Jason here has some information for him." John spoke as they passed the food amongst themselves.

"Jason, I'll take you in. That way, we won't have two cars leaving here." Matt studied Dave's friend, wondering that he hadn't seen him before.

"Works for me. Tell me, though, what excuse are you going to use?"

"Do I need an excuse to go into Mac's for coffee with a friend? Caleb will meet us there. It's already arranged for him to be there early this morning."

Jason shrugged. "Whatever."

Adriel roused as she heard faint footsteps moving around her room. It was morning. For the first time in weeks, she thought, my head's not foggy, and I'm actually hungry.

"Well, well, look's who's awake, Echo. Are you glad, my girl? Are you?"

Adriel turned her head at the voice and frowned. It wasn't Rebecca or Rachel, so who was it?

"Adriel, I don't think we've ever meet formally. I'm Ruth Johnson, from your church. John's been taking care of you and so have I."

"Ruth?" Adriel's voice was just a whisper.

"Here, let me help you sit up a bit and then we'll get some water into you."

"Ruth, what day is it?"

"Day? Well, let's just say you decided to sleep for about three days or so. Not by choice, I might add."

"What do you mean?" Adriel's face showed her apprehension.

"We, or rather, John did, figured out you were still being poisoned and found the right antidote. Now, before you ask, Frankie had to go through your purse. The poison was on your pen and pencil. Someone got to them at some point."

Adriel's head went back and her eyes closed. "I knew it wasn't something I had eaten or drank. Do they know who?"

"Last I heard, they were working on it. Matt had had that doctor from the clinic come in and he had two nurses with you. One of them actually tried to get to your IV, but Matt stopped her. We were brought in to treat you." Ruth sank down onto the edge of the bed and watched Adriel trying to absorb what she was told.

Adriel looked up to find Ruth's eyes on her. "I can tell you who. She's been pretty open with her hatred of me."

"That's what I have heard. A friend of Dave Allison's said the same thing to John. Matt's taken him in to meet with Caleb."

"Murphy? Is there any word?" Adriel was almost pleading in her desperation to find out about him.

Ruth reached for her hand, and Adriel's heart sank. He was dead, she was sure.

"Dave Allison was kidnapped to care for him. God provided a friend in time of need for both of them. They're both same, Adriel. Murphy's with John as is Dave. We'll get you together as soon as we feel it's safe."

Adriel blinked back the tears. "Thank you, Ruth. That will help me to heal even faster."

Ruth stood, dusted her hands together and then headed for the door. "I'll be back with some food for you."

Ian and Joseph were in the kitchen when Ruth entered.

"How is she this morning, Ruth?" Ian's question didn't surprise her in the least. She ha come to know this man and his tender heart.

"Hungry, she tells me. What did you prepare for breakfast this morning, Master Chef?"

Ian laughed at her name for him. "There's some eggs and toast. I doubt you'll want her to have more than that."

"You're so right, Ian. Joseph, now find me a tray while I dish up her breakfast. Oh, there you are, Echo. Go on, girl. Go find Adriel."

Caleb slid into the booth beside Matt and nodded at Jason.

"How's Murphy?" He kept his voice low.

"Getting there. He was awake before I left and John was getting some broth into him. I still can't believe how Jason could get them away."

"Thank you, Jason. Now what was it you wanted to tell me?"

Jason handed Caleb a sheaf of papers. "I've written down everything I can remember. The woman on the board, Adriel's not the first one she's gone after in such a way. She does it though so no one can track her or accuse her. This time, I have the evidence." He handed over a tape. "She tried to get me to help. Someone had put the word out about her. I got to her say openly what she wanted and who she wanted to kill."

Caleb looked down at the tape, then back up at Jason. "Thank you, Jason. This is what we need to arrest her." He stopped, then looked at Matt and back to Jason. "How do Murphy's kidnappers fit it wit her?"

"They don't. They're a separate group. Someone else was after Adriel. I'm working on a name for you, but the group is collectively known as The Compass. Word on the street is that they're also after Abe."

"Abe? Why?"

Jason shrugged. "No one knows. No one is helping them though. Abe and his family are too well liked here in town, always have been." Jason's eyes strayed past the two seated across from them and lost focus.

Matt and Caleb exchanged glances. What had just happened?

Jason brought his glance back to Caleb. "Look for someone named Brent. He's the key to finding the ones who kidnapped Murphy. Like I said, it wasn't just to get to Adriel. If you sent your men out to the old White cottage, you'll find the men still there, I would suspect."

"What did you do, Jason?"

Jason just smiled, then got up and walked away.

"Is he for real, Cale?" Matt's question broke through the quiet that remained.

Caleb nodded as he stood and slid into the other seat. "He is. He's got quite the story if he ever tells it to you. He's good friends with Dave, they were overseas in the same unit." Caleb studied the papers he had stacked tidily on the table and the tape sitting on top of them. "This is going to go a long way to solving one crime, but we still have to find the ones responsible for Murphy's kidnapping. And somehow I don't think that's going to be very easy."

Matt shook his head as he stood. "I don't envy you your job, Caleb. We'll keep you updated on the two."

Caleb found Frankie and handed him the paperwork and tape. "Here's who was after Adriel. We should have enough for an arrest."

Frankie took a swift look through the papers. "It's her, after all. This should be enough. Who?"

"Dave's friend, Jason. Murphy and Dave are safe, thanks to him. I've sent a patrol up to the White cottage. That's where they were being held. Jason again, and I suspect he's done something to prevent the kidnappers from getting away."

"Will this end it, do you think?"

"I suspect not. Jason said there's word on the street someone's after Abe."

"That's what we've been thinking all along. We just have to track down who."

"That we do. I'll leave that with you, Frankie." Caleb walked away.

Frankie stared after him, then turned back to the papers and tape he held. This was one woman he would be glad to see arrested.

Murphy stood, looking out the front window of John's home. John stopped to watch him. He was still a little shaky, John thought, but he's ready to go home. John turned as Dave came towards him.

"Are you set to go home, Dave?"

"More than ready. I've been speaking with my supervisor. I'm not to report for three days." He nodded towards Murphy. "What about him?"

"He's ready to go home but not back to work, not for a while. I'll talk to Abe. You're taking Jason's jeep?"

Dave nodded. "I am. He'll find it when he wants it."

"He's a good friend to you, Dave. He's told me some of what you two went through."

"He doesn't talk much about it."

"Nor do you." He walked towards Murphy. "Murphy, ready to go home?"

Murphy turned, catching his balance as he did. "I am, John. I need to be back home."

"And you need to see Adriel. She's had quite the adventure too. Ruth is with her at Abe's."

It was dusk and Adriel was restless and knew she was feeling better. She stood, perusing Abe's library, trying to find something that would catch her interest and keep her mind of where Murphy was. No one had mentioned him since Ruth had that morning.

A quiet sound came behind her and she froze. When no more noise came, she cautiously turned.

Murphy stood and watched as Adriel turned towards him. He could see the ravages her illness had caused, but to him, she was still beautiful. Her face lighting up joy, she came towards his open arms.

"Murphy, you're here."

"I am, sweetheart. I'm back with you." He drew her down to the couch. "I need to sit, still wobbly."

She tilted her head to study the bandage on the side of his head. "They did a number on you, didn't they?" Her hand reached to gently touch the bruising.

"They did. But it's okay now." He looked towards the doorway. "Caleb needs to talk with us. We're still not safe, you know."

"Will we ever be?"

"Soon, I pray, soon we will be."

Caleb stood in the doorway and watched for a minute, then walked towards them, drawing a chair over to sit down.

"Adriel, it's good to see you back up and on your feet."

"It is good, Caleb. I didn't realize how sick I was."

"No one did. Murphy, how's the head?"

Murphy shrugged. "It's there. What more can I say?"

Caleb shook his head at the two of them. "Adriel, to start with you. Tammy Brett has been arrested and charged with attempted murder. She's not saying why. The team's searching her house. It's more than just what went out about the shelter.

"I sent a team out to where you were held, Murphy. Your kidnappers were still there, thanks to Jason. Not the brightest people, not thinkers or problem solvers I would say. They're not saying why or who, other than Adriel was not the real target in kidnapping you, Murphy. They were to make it look like it was, but you were the primary target."

"Murphy? Why?"

"That's what we're trying to find out, Adriel. None of them are talking either. It's going to be a long investigation, the way it's going so far."

"I can tell you why, Caleb." Eddie walked into the room.

"Eddie, what did you find out?"

"Lots. We finally tracked down the information we were looking for on Tammy Brett. She's related to the leader who kidnapped Murphy. He's her brother, Andrew. She finally talked as well. She had tried to kill Adriel and when that didn't work, hired her brother to try. He decided that to do so, he needed to get to Murphy. I'm not sure how they got past the security here. My feeling is that they had help somewhere."

"I'm sure they did, Eddie. We just have to find out who and why."

"So, how do we find this guy or whoever it is? I won't feel safe until we do." Adriel eyes searched between the two men facing her. She could feel Murphy's arm tighten around her/

"That's what we're working on, Adriel. For now, I would suggest you go back to what you were doing. It's the only way that you can start to feel safe again, is to reclaim your life."

Murphy stared at Caleb. "Just like that, Caleb, go back to her normal life?"

Caleb stared Murphy down. "I know you don't like it, Murphy, but right now, we can't provide protection for her. Your team's heading out in a few days. We can't keep her locked up."

Sensing her mistress' agitation, Echo had jumped up to join her on the couch. Chin on Adriel's knee, her brown eyes watched intently. Adriel dug her fingers in the white fur of the ruff.

"You're right, Caleb. I do need to get on with what I was doing." She stopped, staring into the distance. "I have a name I would like you to check out, someone from my past. He may be the one behind it all." She handed him a slip of paper, having been prepared for one of them to come out. She absolutely refused to say his name.

"What makes you think he has found you?"

She shrugged. "I don't know. Just what's been happening, especially with Murphy, seems more like him than Tammy. I can see her poisoning someone but kidnapping where she could be tied to that? Not happening."

"Are you telling me our investigation is off base?" Eddie spoke quietly, eyes intent on her.

"No, Eddie, I don't. I think somehow it's all connected in a bizarre way."

After the two officer had left, Murphy turned to her. "Are you really planning to go back in to your office?"

She nodded, then rose, walking away from him. "I have to, Murphy. If I don't have your support in this, then I guess we're just not ready for this." She pulled the ring from her finger and dropped it onto Abe's desk, walking from the room.

Murphy rose and went towards the desk. Had she really just done that? Lord, what am I to do with her? She needs protection but is refusing it. He picked up the ring, pocketed and went to find her.

"Adriel, we need to talk. You didn't give me a chance to say anything. That decision affects both of us?"

She spun, eyes flashing at him. "Not any more."

He stood for a minute, then went towards her where she stood by the window in her room.

"Adriel, stop. We need to talk. We'll work this through. I wasn't questioning whether you should or not. I just wanted to be sure that you would be safe."

She turned, finding him close behind her. Taking a step backwards, she looked up at him, tears sparkling in her eyes.

"Murphy, I don't want you hurt again. I can't handle that."

Hands on her shoulders, he studied her face. "We could be married and one of us hit by a car and die. There are no guarantees of anything, except that God loves us and desires to protect us. Sometimes that protection is taking us home to Him. Can you live with that? You know my job can be dangerous. I just never expected to have danger target you like it has from your work." He reached for her hand and slid the ring back on it. "Leave it there, please. We'll work through this."

Chapter 26

He watched as the police detectives searched the woman's house and cursed. How had they found her? Now he had lost his source of information in town. How was he to get to Adriel now? He turned and walked towards the downtown area. She had an office there. Maybe he could find her there by herself.

Adriel stood in the room she had chosen for her own office and looked around. She was only working part days still, but her work load was growing. It had been two weeks since Murphy had been found and he was back at work, worrying about her every time she came to town. She shook her head. Today, she moved back to her own home. It was time. Murphy was starting to hover and smother and she didn't want that.

Lord, keep them safe, she prayed. The team was heading out that day for a week-long security assignment, Murphy had said.

She turned to her paperwork. There were just so many people that are hurting, Lord. How do I help the few I can?

Hours later, she roused from her work, realizing it was starting to get dark. Packing up what she needed, she headed for the door and hesitated. Something stopped her from using the front door, a strong sense of danger. She retraced her steps to the back door. That was better, she thought. She cautiously opened the door and stepped out. It looked clear. She hastened her steps towards her car, unlocking it just as she got to it, and slipped inside. The doors locked once again, she pulled away from the back of the building. She could feel someone watching her but couldn't see who it was.

I don't want to go home, Lord. Who do I go to? She drove around aimlessly for a while. This is ridiculous, she thought. I'm jumping at nothing. She turned towards the suburbs. She knew who she could go to.

Ringing the doorbell of the house, she waited, eyes restlessly scanning the area around her. She felt safe, didn't she? She no longer had that sense of peace though, that she had always had in this town.

Peg Brown stood at the open door, watching Adriel. Eddie had warned her she might show up,

"Adriel, come. Into the house with you." Peg reached for her and pulled her inside. "What are you doing here?"

Adriel shook her head. "I'm sorry, Peg. I shouldn't have come but it felt like someone was waiting for me when I went to leave work. I wasn't sure where I should go."

"You've come to the right place. Have you had your supper yet? No? Come with me. You can help. Eddie's on his way home and I could use some help finishing off the meal/"

"Are you sure, Peg?"

"I am. Now into the kitchen with you."

Peg heard Eddie's key in the lock and went to meet him.

"Adriel's here, Eddie. She's running scared but trying hard not to show it."

His keen eyes studied his wife's face. "I thought we might see her. She's still trying to work through some names. Did she say what happened?"

Peg shook her head. "Other than saying she felt like someone was waiting for her when she went to leave work, and that she shouldn't have come here, nothing."

Eddie nodded. "She is being watched by someone. We're tracing back through all the information we were given, but it's tedious. Come on, Peg-of-my-heart. Let's go face our house guest."

Adriel looked up from the counter she was working at, a hesitant smile on her face.

Eddie stood and watched her for a moment, then spoke. "Welcome to our home, Adriel. It's your home for as long as you want."

They could see the visible relation in her tension as she spoke. "Thank you, Eddie. I wasn't sure if I should have come here."

"It's what you were told to do. Now, what have you ladies come up with for supper?" Eddie walked past Adriel, briefly laying a hand on her shoulder, then headed for the stove to see what Peg had created for them.

Eddie watched Adriel as she walked restlessly around the living room, finally speaking. "Adriel, come sit. Tell me what's going on."

She turned to look at him, sighing as she plopped down into a chair. "I don't know, Eddie. The feeling of danger was just so high today when I went to leave work. I'm not sure any more who I can and can't trust. Does that make sense?"

"Perfect sense. Now, tell me what are you going to do about it?"

Her eyes met his steady ones. "I've been doing a lot of thinking. I need to find a realtor. I can't go back to that house. I'll have to find somewhere I can stay that I can take Echo."

"Don't worry about Echo. I know a couple of ladies who will gladly board her for you. They have Shelties as well."

"Oh, that would be wonderful. I need to confront this fellow, or whoever it is, Eddie, and I'm not sure how to."

Eddie nodded. "Figured it was something like that. What are your thoughts?"

"Other than keeping Murphy away from me, I haven't thought of a lot."

"Okay. That one'll be difficult, I'm sure you understand."

"I do." She looked back at him and then at Peg. "What do I do? I have some thoughts but I'm not sure how they'll work out."

"Let's hear your thoughts and then we'll get it figured out. In the mean while, I'll go collect your dog once we're finished. Ashling Bradley will take her or Caleb's sister-in-law, Laycee, will."

Finally, Adriel sat back. "Will this work, do you think, Eddie?"

"We'll give it our best shot. We'll get him, Adriel."

"I wish I had your confidence, Eddie. But I don't. I feel like he's going to get away, and my life will always be on hold."

Eddie watched as she stood and walked back through to the kitchen, to find Peg. He rose and headed for the door. He was going to collect her dog, then pay Caleb a visit. Caleb would not be happy, he knew, but that was life. Adriel had made her decision, decided to include them. She could have very easily not.

Chapter 27

Murphy sat in his truck, staring at Adriel's, stunned at the sold sign on the lawn. What had happened in the ten days they were gone? The house looked empty, no window treatments, porch bare. Where was she?

He headed for her office and trying the door, got no answer. It didn't look as if anyone had been there in a couple of days. Her work cell went to voice mail. Her personal cell as well. Where are you, Adriel? Murphy stood and stared around. Where did you go to?

He finally made his way to Mac's, why he wasn't sure. He didn't know where else to go. Mac saw him as he entered, came towards him and sent him back to his office. Mac watched as he headed that way, his heart breaking for his young friend. He turned, searching the cafe. There, Ian was still here and by himself.

Mac stopped by Ian's table. "Ian, can you come back to my office? Murphy's here."

Ian stood and followed him. "Murphy? Where's Adriel?"

Mac shrugged. "I just think you need to be with your friend." He reached for an envelope he had tucked under the cash register. "Give him this."

Ian took the envelope, studying the single word "Murphy" on it. He nodded, then headed towards the office. He stopped, eyes on

Murphy. He read the devastation, hurt, worry, and whatever emotions Murphy feeling just in the way he was slumped into the chair. He dropped into a chair beside him and said nothing.

Finally, he spoke, "You okay, Murphy?"

Murphy shook his head. "I can't find her, Ian. Her house is sold. She's not at her office. Neither phone is answered."

Ian nodded, then handed over the envelope Mac had handed him.

"What's this?" Murphy was puzzled.

"I don't know. Mac just handed it to me when he sent me back here. That's Adriel's writing, isn't it?"

Murphy ran his thumb over the writing and nodded, unable to speak. He stared the envelope, not wanting to open it.

"It's not going to bite, Murphy. It's better that you know what she says." Ian pushed himself to his feet, sorrow in his heart for his friend.

"No, Ian, stay. I'd rather you did."

Ian sat back down, eyes narrowing as he searched Murphy's profile. "Are you sure? That's likely pretty personal."

"It can't be any more personal that it already is."

Murphy turned the envelope over and over, finally reaching for the sealed flap. Pulling it open, he hesitated before removing the single folded sheet of paper.

He still hesitated before he unfolded it. Lord, I have no idea what's on this, or what she has to say. You do. Prepare my heart, Lord, for whatever it says.

He finally unfolded the piece of paper, tears blurring his vision. He blinked, clearing his eyes to read.

Dearest Murphy,

Please do not hate me. I have had to take this step, this step without you, to flush out whoever it is that is behind my troubles. I had hoped it would be all over and done with by the time you got back, but if you're reading this, it means it isn't and Mac has found you.

I have an idea who is it and am taking steps to bring him out of hiding. If you're reading this, you will see my house has sold. It sold quicker than I thought it would. I wanted to tell you, dear one, that I was putting it up for sale, but you were away, and I wouldn't disturb you just for this. He will try to get to me again through you, and I can't and won't have you hurt again, not for anything. Echo is safe. I made sure of that. She will be yours if something happens to me.

Peg has our ring. I have left it with her for safekeeping. Eddie and Peg have helped me keep my head on straight and true to the course

I have laid out. Eddie can contact me only if it's an absolute emergency. Talk to him, dear one. He will help you get through this. They have welcomed me in as a daughter to their home and hearts and have us covered with constant prayer.

Know that I love you deeply, Murphy. You are the one who has helped to keep me sane during all this. You have constantly sent me back to God, to seek His peace. Keep that peace within you, Murphy.

Where can I run to, Murphy, where he can't find me? There is nowhere I can go. He is all around me, no matter where I step or stop. Take care, Murphy. Don't let him get close to you again.

I don't know how this will end, Murphy. My desire is that it is over quickly and we're together again. If not, then know you have all my love and that God has decided it is time for me to graduate to heaven.

All my love and prayers.

Adriel

Murphy blinked away the tears at he finished, a finger tracing her name. Adriel, I wish you had waited for me. I want to be where you are. Lord, keep her safe. Help me to feel the peace she so desired I do.

Ian watched the conflicting emotions crossing Murphy's face. "Is she okay, Murphy?"

Murphy shrugged as he folded the letter and tucked it back into the envelope, then into his pocket. "I don't know, Ian. She's decided to face whoever this on her own."

"On her own?" Ian was stunned. "No one with her?"

"Not by the sounds of it. She does mention that Eddie can get in touch with her if needed. I want to talk with him." He rose and Ian laid a hand on his arm.

"Just be careful, Murphy. You're back and they can still get to her through you. Joseph's out in the cafe. I came with him. Let me go with you."

Murphy hesitated, then nodded. Of all his team mates, Ian understood him the best. They were often teamed up together. This was one time, though, that his negotiation skills wouldn't work. He had no idea where Adriel was or if she was even safe.

Eddie looked up as Murphy and Ian stood in his office doorway. He looked past them, then stood and motioned them in, closing the door behind him. His eyes on Murphy, he sat back down into his chair.

Murphy's eyes never left his. "Where is she, Eddie?"

Eddie hesitated. "I gather Mac found you."

Murphy nodded. "I read her letter. Where is she?"

"It won't work, Murphy."

"What won't?"

"Finding her.   I don't even know where she is. She took off during the night a couple of days ago and neither Peg or I have seen her. She's picked up a lot on how to survive from the ladies she worked with."

Murphy nodded, still staring at Eddie. "Can you find her?"

Eddie shook his head. "I promised her I wouldn't unless it was life and death. So far it isn't. I can't break that trust, Murphy, no matter what."

Murphy finally nodded, Ian watching him closely. "What was she planning?"

"She never really said. She had a number of ideas but she never confirmed which one she would try. She's still in town, Murphy, as far as I know. Her car is locked in my garage. Her furniture and belongings we tucked away into storage for her. Echo is with Laycee and Joshua Logan." He studied his young friend. "You really had no idea she'd try this?"

Murphy shook his head this time. "No, I didn't, Eddie. I just wish she had told me."

"She was too worried about you, Murphy, to do that. It almost killed her, along with the poison, when you went missing." He looked down, then looked up at Ian, who was staring at Murphy.   "I wish I could help you more, Murphy, but I just don't know where she is.

We're still working through the investigation, but we haven't got all the pieces yet."

Murphy stood abruptly and began pacing, deep in thought. Then he stopped, eyes closing. "I know where she is." He pulled out the letter she had written. "She won't come right out and say it but it's there."

"Where, Murphy?"

Murphy shook his head. "I need to go there on my own. That's the only way she'll meet me."

Murphy turned and strode from the office, Ian on his heels. Eddie stared after them, then shook his head. Wherever Murphy thought Adriel was, she not likely was. He looked up as Frankie appeared.

"Wasn't that Murphy and Ian?" He stared back out the door.

Eddie sighed. "It was. Murphy's discovered Adriel gone into hiding and thinks he knows where to find her."

"And does he?"

Eddie shrugged. "Where do we stand in the investigation?"

"Adriel's good. She pinpointed the name that we've been looking for."

"She did? Now that's interesting. How'd she manage that?"

"That's what I'd like to know." Frankie
handed over the paper. "This is where he was
last seen, but he's gone from there. We're
tracking him now."

Chapter 28

"Are you sure about this, Murphy?" Abe studied him as he stuffed food and water bottles into a knapsack.

"No, I'm not but it's the only thing that makes sense." He pulled out his letter and read,

"Where can I run to, Murphy, where he can't find me? There is nowhere I can go. He is all around me, no matter where I step or stop. Take care, Murphy. Don't let him get close to you again.

"That tells me she's somewhere around here."

Abe thought about what she had said. "It makes sense in a sort of way. But if she's wrong or you're wrong, then what?"

"If I'm not back in twelve hours, come looking for me. She knows about the cabin behind us. I told her about it one day. I didn't think she'd ever take this step."

"None of us did." Abe turned to watch the rest of the team walking towards them, shoulder to shoulder, almost matching in height, a formidable wall of manpower. "What do you want us to do?"

Murphy turned, seeing his friends walking towards them. "I don't know, Abe. To tell you the truth, I'm not even sure she's there. I'm just following an impression I have."

"Sometimes, that's how we do it." Abe stopped speaking, then reached to drop something in Murphy's hand. "Use this tracker. It will help us know where you are. And we're not waiting twelve hours. If you're not back in six, we're following you. Sooner if we can any word at all you two are in danger. Got that?"

Murphy nodded, shared a glance with each team member, then turned and walked away.

Matt spoke up. "Where's he headed?"

"The old cabin. He thinks she's there."

"How long do we give him?" This from Joseph.

"I told him six hours, but I don't like that. Get ready. We'll move out as soon as we can."

The men scattered, making for their equipment and supplies.

Murphy cautiously approached the cabin, stopping every few feet to stare around and listen. He couldn't hear anything, but then he didn't expect to. He reached for the cabin door, then stopped and turned, feeling eyes on him. Who was out there? He turned and made his way around to the back of the building, and stood waiting. Ears straining to hear, his heart beating faster than normal in anticipation, every little rustle and noise was someone out there, ready to come for them. He finally reached for the door at the back of the cabin, quietly pushing it open.

His eyes adjusting to the dimness, he dropped his pack beside the door and looked around. He was right. Adriel had been here, but where was she? The smallest whisper of sound had him ducking and turning as a heavy branch swung at his head.

He picked himself up from the floor and grasped the branch, turning the person wielding it towards him.

"Adriel, it's me. Murphy."

Adriel dropped the branch "Murphy! Why are you here? I didn't want you here."

Murphy reached for her, pulling her into his arms. "That's too bad. I'm here. Now tell me what you're planning?"

A mutinous look on her face, she broke way from him. "No. Now leave. It won't work if he knows you're here."

"What won't work and just who is he?"

"I will be glad to tell him, Adriel."

They both spun as the front door of the cabin was shoved open and a man entered, a man not tall in stature and wizened and frail.

Murphy shoved Adriel behind him. "Who are you?"

"Has she never told you? Tsk, tsk, Adriel. That's a shame." He looked at her with a sneer on his face. "You never would admit you knew me, would you?"

"Adriel?" Murphy's voice held a question but she heard his confidence in her underlying it.

"This man? He was a teacher I had in high school. No one liked him. He decided I would be his "project", that he would mould me to take over his little empire of theft and drugs and blackmail he had running. He grew violent when I refused and moved away. I had suspected he was tracking me. I guess he was."

"And because you went to the authorities, I ended up in prison for 10 years. It's taken me four years to find you. Now, you'll pay for what you did."

"I don't think so. You see, the police already have your name and description and your last known address. They have the documents from the court case. They have my statement. If anything happens to me, then you'll pay in a bigger way. They've connected you to the attack and kidnapping of Murphy and Dave. How did you fall so far?"

A weapon was raised at pointed and pointe at them, as shaky as the man's hand who held it.

Murphy's eyes narrowed as he caught a glimpse of movement outside the door. Abe hadn't waited. He didn't think he would and he was right. Now he had to distract this maniac before he discharged the weapon. As shaky as his hand was, who knew where the bullets would end up.

"Adriel, step back a bit." Murphy's voice was low and he barely moved his lips. He felt her step back slowly and more behind him. Good, he thought. Now we have room to move if we need too. Lord, I need my negotiation skills to work, and I'm not sure they will.

Murphy continued to talk, prying into the events of the past, getting the old man to talk more and more openly. He knew he had people outside who were listening. What he didn't know was that Eddie and Frankie and four other officers were there as well.

Finally, his frustration at a level he could no longer control, his weapon steadied as best he could in two hands, he pointed it at Murphy's heart.

"Enough! No more talk! You both die!"

"Adriel, drop!" Murphy's voice rang through the cabin as he dropped, landing on his hands, and his feet swinging around to hit the man in the back of the legs. The weapon discharged as the man went down.

The cabin filled with men as Murphy rose to his feet and sought Adriel. Stooping, he gathered her into his arms and strode out the door, sinking to the ground, his back against the chopping block. Adriel clung to him, then sat up

"Is it over, Murphy? Is it really over?"

He nodded, eyes on her face. "It is, Adriel. It finally is." His eyes rose to see Eddie standing in front of him. "It is over, isn't it, Eddie?"

"It is, Murphy.   Thanks to Adriel, we have him. Who knows when we would have caught him if she hadn't taken this step. It was him all along. Never her foster family." Eddie stared down at them, then turned to walk away. "Don't forget to come see Peg for your ring."

Epilogue

Adriel looked around the cabin she and Murphy had chosen for their own. It was not the one Murphy currently had. Abe had told them to decorate, make any renovations they wanted, and sent him the bill. He had had a good friend with a landscaping business put up privacy fencing for them.

She was content. Her work as a paralegal. advocating for women and children, was starting to take off. She had become deeply involved in the church they attended, something she had never done before.

Arms came around her from behind, and she leaned back against Murphy's strong body. He dropped a kiss on her hair.

"What are you thinking about so hard?" Murphy's voice ruffled the hair near her ear.

"Just being thankful, Murphy. God has blessed us with so much."

"He has, Adriel. In so many ways."

"You're more peaceful, Murphy, more than you used to be. I see God at work in you."

"He is. One of those verses that you and I clung to has really resonated with me, or I should say two."

"And they are?"

"That we have the peace that Christ left for us and that God is in control, knowing that His plans and purposes are so much better than ours."

"That they are, Murphy." She turned to face him. "Now, we have to set a date you know. Everyone's asking. Eddie has already asked if he can escort me up the aisle to you. Peg has offered me her wedding gown. She was saving it for their daughter, but that little one didn't live."

"They are really a wonderful couple, Adriel. I'm glad you have them in your life." He reached for her hand. "Okay, so let's go find a calendar. Greg Evans will be busy just with our team if the trend continues."

She laughed. "He will be at that, and he will enjoy every minute of it."

She stopped and stared up at the tall man she loved so deeply. "When I thought I had lost you, I thought my life was over. God showed me differently. I want that difference to come through in my work and in how we interact with others."

He stooped to kiss her. "And it will. God is already working that way, my love. Now let's find that calendar and get everyone off our backs about a date."

"We could always elope, you know."

Murphy started laughing. "That won't work. They'd just follow us wherever we ran to."

Dear Readers:

Thank you for choosing to read the story of Murphy and Adriel. It is my prayer that you too will find the peace that only God can offer and that you come to realize that He has plans and purposes for our lives we never know about. How many times have you started along the road of life and been shot off on a tangent? Many, I would suspect, if your life is anything like mine.

My parents firmly believed that God has a purpose for each one of us and a plan for each one. Dad would often talk about being in Egypt or the desert when he should have been where God wanted him to be. We have a tendency to wander away and wander back. God always has us in His care.

May you find that place and peace where God would have you to be. I'm still working on finding mine, and part of mine now seems to be writing. God is providing the words and there are days my fingers just aren't fast enough to keep up with what He's dictating.

A thank you once again to my faithful friend and sister in Christ, Faye Silvestro Kubassek, who takes the time to proofread each and every book I write. I'd be lost without you, sis.

God bless each one of you.

Ronna